PETTY ROOTS

A Summer Wedding in Solberg

PETTY ROOTS

Cozy DuBois

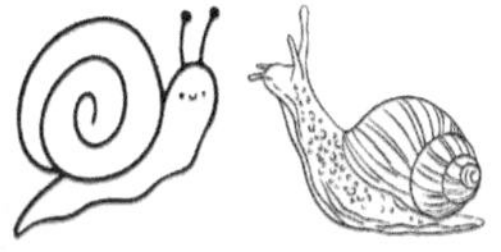

To the outcasts and petty bitches.
And in memory of Luke.

Author's Note

Welcome to Solberg—a fictional small town in Minnesota that is home to a handful of queer and trans oddballs, who struggle to fit in (as many of us do). Small towns are not always kind to people who stick out, and this series explores the discomfort about the people who are just a bit too weird for the typical cozy romance novel. Everyone belongs in Solberg and deserves to call it home, whether their neighbors like it or not. Join our protagonists as they navigate the most confusing of heteronormative traditions: marriage. Not their own—that would be too simple to play by their own rules. No, our dear characters are attending other people's weddings!

Admittedly, this is an odd pitch for the commonality in a series of interconnected romance standalones, but hear me out! This series was inspired by my own experiences as a nonbinary and neurodivergent wedding officiant. I've seen so many unique traditions and fraught family dynamics, and all of them are fascinating and magical. While I haven't fallen in love with anyone at a wedding (yet!), there's something intriguing about a cultural milestone dedicated to love and commitment while also being deeply entrenched in rituals that pressure people to perform gender and emotions the correct way. The potential for romance is magnified by the magic of a wedding!

A quick note on the representation in this book: as a queer and trans author, my goal is to write LGBTQ+ characters who feel real. As such, any on-page exposition about labels or pronouns is minimal and sometimes only implied, presuming that the other characters are familiar with the concepts and each other.

The main characters in *Petty Roots* prefer fluid, intersectional labels that represent the openness of their sexuality and gender. Blake is trans masc (someone who leans masculine but does not necessarily identify as a man), and Eris identifies most closely with genderfuck (someone who intentionally subverts the traditional gender binary through gender expression, identity, or presentation). They both identify with the labels trans, non-binary, bisexual, and queer, though not necessarily in the same way or to the same degree. Additionally, both main characters use non-gendered pronouns (Blake: they/them/their/themself, Eris: ze/zim/zis/zimself), even if not every side character uses them perfectly.

Additionally, Blake is not aware they may be autistic (Eris has a hunch, though!), but displays several neurodivergent traits, such as alexithymia, auditory processing issues, and difficulty navigating social cues. The possibility is not discussed in the main story, as I wasn't intending to make Blake autistic-coded, but whoops! Another accidentally neurodivergent character.

I hope you enjoy the story and find the characters as honest and complicated and delightful as I do. Thank you for supporting this odd little series, because I have so many stories waiting to be told about summer weddings on Solberg!

Content Awareness

Brief references to terrorist organizations and government agencies (the KKK, ICE, and the DEA). The story was written before the 2024 election and revisions were originally completed in early 2025. While these organizations have always been a concern to Latine-Americans and other racialized groups in the United States, the characters in this series exist outside of the context of our current timeline, and the story is not meant to not reflect on our lived reality today. (And a huge, resounding "Fuck ICE!" from this Minneapolis-based author.)

- Explicit sex scenes with minor degradation: PIV and oral sex between two non-binary people, with on-page discussion to ensure their encounters are gender-affirming.

- Internalized and external ableism: includes references to a past car accident that resulted in major injury and long term impacts (physical and psychological), and a conversation with a grandparent who has dementia.

- Substance use: alcohol and marijuana, references to psilocybin.

- Transphobia: ranges from a supportive parent who doesn't quite get it to dehumanizing language, intentional misgendering, and deadnaming.

For more details on the possible triggers (including spoilers), please visit cozydubois.com.

One

THE ENVELOPE

ONE HOUR AND FORTY-FOUR minutes in, and my morning study block is as good as wasted. Unable to make sense of a single word of this case study, I glare at my laptop, as if my vacuous state is entirely the computer's fault. My head is too full—of doubt, hesitation, and perhaps guilt—to focus. Despite my best efforts, my eyes keep drifting to the pink envelope on the coffee table, sitting innocently on a pile of textbooks—

A chime from the train station outside makes me jump, and I shake my head. "Sixteen minutes left." Squinting and blinking through the storm behind my eyes, I stare blankly at incomprehensible legalese, hoping it'll magically click. After two years of law school, I should be used to pushing myself. The nagging feeling that maybe I'm not cut out to be a lawyer eats away—

My phone lights up, and the steady buzz on the coffee table brings welcome relief.

With a huff, I scramble to answer. My mom calling is a convenient excuse to give up on pretending to study. Becoming a lawyer has been my primary objective for four years; I just need a break. This inner doubt stems from the mental bedlam caused by this damn envelope, that's all.

Stretching my neck, I practice a convincing smile and hit accept. Mom's calls always include video; she needs evidence that I'm not miserable and living in squalor. Carefully, I angle the phone away from the clutter and the half-eaten food left out on the kitchenette behind me, just as her face pops on the screen. The haphazard stacks of textbooks behind me are just as messy as the rest of my apartment, but she'll be happier with a view of my bookshelf. "Hey, Mom."

"Morning, Blakey-poo!" Mom beams, though I can only see the smile in her eyes because of how close the phone is to her face. Her messy bun of frizzy red hair takes up most of the screen; she cares more about seeing me up close than how she looks. "How's my favorite daugh—sorry, adult offspring doing on this beautiful Saturday morning?"

I fight to keep my smile bright. At least she caught herself today. My mother tries, even if she doesn't quite get it. "I'm good. How are you?"

Mom tsks, endearingly dramatic as always. "I'll be better when your father gets back. I want my cinnamon roll!"

My dad is presumably the cinnamon roll she's referencing, but I choose to believe my mother is talking about baked goods. That's my parents' Saturday routine: Dad drives to the middle of nowhere at the ass crack of dawn to sit by himself in silence and bird-watch, then picks up cinnamon rolls on his way back when loud people start scaring the birds away by midmorning. I miss those quiet mornings with Dad in the woods and wetlands, watching the sun rise and the world awaken. I miss Mom's comfortable chatter, the aroma of fresh coffee while inhaling a cinnamon roll larger than my head.

"What are you up to today?" Mom asks, startling me out of my memories.

"Studying." Same answer as always, except for the additional, "Exams are next week."

Mom tsks again, this time in disappointment. Her sound effects are their own language. "I love how dedicated you are, Blake, but remember to relax too! Enjoy the city while you have the chance to live there."

My face freezes into the nice mask Mom prefers, but inside, I'm squirming. *This* conversation should be avoided. She's half-right; I've barely explored Chicago in the two years I've lived here, and I don't want to move back to Minnesota before I've given myself a chance to enjoy it.

Or ever.

But Mom isn't ready for the whole *I'm actually not moving back* talk. I should probably tell her I already have a job lined up. Though whether I can keep it is contingent on if I pass the bar, and she knows my lease isn't up until September. So really, I can delay that uncomfortable conversation for at least a month. Maybe two. "I am! I'm actually going to brunch with Adrienne in a few."

For my mom's peace of mind, Adrienne is my new best friend. In reality, I barely know her, though I'm closer with her than anyone else in Chicago. Adrienne took me under her wing during orientation, and she's kept me there since. It's unclear if she's merely being nice to the only other queer person in our law school cohort, or if she actually likes me.

Making friends as an adult, even a grad student, is very different from making friends in undergrad or high school. I haven't quite got the hang of it, not that I was ever that great at it back in Solberg either. Adrienne's monthly invites to brunch, with her other misfit queer friends, are my lifeline to a semblance of a social life in Chicago.

"Oh, that sounds lovely! You were always such a social butterfly!"

I snort. I've *never* been a social butterfly. *Matt* was a social butterfly; he always dragged me along with him when we were kids. And the only friend I made in college was Allie.

"Are you going to fix your hair before you go? It looks like you could use a trim."

Self-conscious, I fluff the soft black curls on my forehead and squint at my tiny picture on the phone. "I just got it cut last weekend."

"Oh. You're growing it out again? That's great, sweetie!" Mom squeals. "You always looked so pretty with your long curls! I told you that pixie cut didn't suit you, and now look, you practically have a mullet until it grows out again. Maybe they could do some layers next time you go?"

I swallow the defensive sarcasm that bubbles in my chest, like a burp that would be *so* satisfying to let rip. My mullet is intentional, and my "pixie cut" was a buzz cut. But Mom prefers to interpret my appearance through women's styles. When I came out as non-binary three years ago, she said she loved and supported me no matter what. It was the same speech she gave when I came out as bi in high school. But apparently, that hasn't extended to hair.

I must take too long to respond because Mom hums, her signal that she's changing the subject. "Anyway, I was calling to check in. See how you're holding up with the news?"

"News?" I squawk. News isn't a good word. There should be no news coming from Solberg. "What news?"

Mom exhales through her teeth, which makes me more nervous; that's *Dad's* nervous tick when he's avoiding a sensitive subject. "You know...about Mattie and Allie. Their wedding?"

"Oh." That's not news. That's been coming. I've known they would get married since I moved to Chicago two years ago. In the small town of Solberg, Minnesota—where I was raised and stayed for college—I left behind my two best friends: my high school sweetheart and my college roommate. In my absence, the boy next door (who didn't want to do long-distance) grew even closer to my bubbly roomie, who stayed with my parents after graduation for an internship. By the time summer was over, Matt and Allie had moved in together.

Which I was *totally* fine with.

They announced their engagement in the group chat six months ago, and their other friends got invitations two months ago. *I* didn't get one. But everyone else gushed about how pretty and perfect the invites were. Again, *totally* support them and their choices, even the choice to not invite me.

So their wedding is not "news". I've just been choosing not to talk about it. Or think about it. Because it didn't concern me.

At least, until I got the mail yesterday.

"You know, the Jacobsons didn't want to invite us?" Mom tsks again, this time in disgust. My parents and Matt's parents (despite being next-door neighbors since Matt and I were in diapers) do not get along. The Jacobsons aren't bad people, but they're a little obsessed with normalcy. And that's not my family. Allie—all five-foot-two, feminine, sweet, blonde, and painfully straight—is going to be a much better daughter-in-law than my queer, trans-masc ass ever would have been.

Love that for them.

"Mattie and Allie hand-delivered us an invite when they came over for Family Friday Game Night, since the other one had gotten 'lost in the mail,'" Mom scoffs. "Sounds like someone made damn *sure* it got lost in the mail. Allie said they were sending you another one too, since they hadn't gotten your RSVP either. Did you get it?"

Boy, did I! The blush envelope, perfectly lovely and traditional with eucalyptus leaves, woven texture, gold accents and so so so *pink*, has been burning a hole in my brain since it arrived yesterday.

"I'll have to check the mail," I lie as I stare the damn thing down, desperate to avoid answering the inevitable question of whether or not I'll attend. "Are you gonna go?"

Mom sighs. "No. Your father and I talked about it, and we still have to live next door to the Jacobsons. Mattie hinted that his parents didn't know we were invited, and frankly, we just came to a truce about the chickens. I don't want to get them riled up again. Your father almost quit Facebook because of her passive-aggressive bullshit in the Solberg Townie group. And you know he loves his Facebook."

My father does love his Facebook. Luckily for bird-watching groups, instead of the usual things middle-aged dads love Facebook for.

"I invented some excuse about a vacation, so now we're road-tripping to New Mexico to check some wildlife refuge off your father's bucket list. He wants to see a road-runner!"

Well, if my parents aren't going, maybe I could safely open the envelope. Just to RSVP no. Because I'm not supposed to go to their wedding. I'm the ex. Exes don't go to weddings. Even if they've been best friends since they were five. Or roommates since freshman year, who clicked on a soulmate-level of clicking.

Admittedly, it hurt, not getting an invite when everyone else did. Far worse than I expected it to. I thought my happiness for the two people I love most in the world (my parents excluded)—and who loved me more than anyone (again, other than my parents)—would outweigh the bitterness of them starting a life together.

Because I always imagined that their life would still include me.

Even though I know I'm not meant for them. Matt knew it. Allie knew it. But I was the one in denial. Matt made that decision for us. Now he and Allie have a life that's theirs, even though I *always* made room for Allie in the life I had with Matt.

But I've processed and accepted their choices. I support them and their relationship, and I wish them nothing but love and light and happiness.

"You should still go though!"

"What?" That's not what Mom was supposed to say.

"You should go!" Mom says with forced nonchalance. "They're your best friends! It would mean a lot if you went. I know things have been awkward since... Well, you know."

Since my boyfriend of eight years broke up with me and almost immediately started dating my best friend? Yeah, it's been awkward.

"Yeah, but I don't want to make their wedding awkward." I shrug, fighting the urge to hug myself. More so, I don't want to feel awkward at their wedding. All of their guests my age are Matt's friends, a few Allie's. None of Matt's friends have bothered to keep in touch, unless not kicking me out of their group chat counts as keeping in touch. To Allie's friends, I was just her weird and quiet roommate, or worse, their professor's kid.

"Blakey-poo, *you* won't make their wedding awkward. *Their families* are going to make it awkward! Mattie is like a son to us, but boy, I am really glad you're not marrying into that family. You dodged a fucking bullet!" Mom sighs dramatically. "If I didn't think they'd clutch their pearls so hard they'd choke, I would give them some of our fun candy in a heartbeat. I've never met anyone who likes having a stick up their ass as much as the Jacobsons do."

My parent's "fun candies" are psilocybin chocolates Mom gets from one of her students at Sigurdsson College. Dad's homegrown strain of weed, perfected over decades to help Dad manage his pain and Mom's anxiety, is popular with the Siggys. As a philosophy professor (obviously tenured), Mom believes it's safer to supply the student body with something trustworthy, so they don't turn to shadier sources. She barters instead of selling, and only off-campus, as if that makes it somehow more acceptable.

The Jacobsons would lose their shit if they knew their hippie neighbors—who don't mow their lawn, and let their chickens run loose, and support their queer kid—are potheads. Even though that should be obvious. Dad has the weird, scraggly, middle-aged man ponytail and wears cargo vests. And Mom is literally Ms. Frizzle, if Ms. Frizzle taught philosophy at a private liberal arts college.

A calendar notification dips across my mother's hair, a reminder that I have an excuse to get off the phone (the necessary first step when it comes to ending phone calls with my mom, or she'll keep talking for hours). "Oh, gotta go, Mom. Need to get ready for brunch."

"Oh yeah! Where are you going?"

"Umm...Some diner." The fewer details, the better.

I'm actually going to a drag brunch in Boystown, and while my mom is cool, she's not *that* cool. She understands the bisexual thing, and supports me no matter what (which I do not take for granted), but drag seems to rub her second-wave feminist principles the wrong way. Same reason I don't push her to compliment my increasingly masc presentation, even though she bends over backwards looking for anything femme to gush about. And why I tell her that she/her pronouns don't bother me that much (even though they do). My mom is not ready to unpack her gender essentialism, and I'm too much of a people pleaser to push her. If I tell her I'm going to a drag show now, she's going to want to have a Long Conversation about it.

"Well, I'll let you get going then, I just wanted to call and see how you're doing."

Step two: the summary of what we already talked about. "Yeah, just busy studying." As usual.

"And you'll think about going to that wedding?"

"If I get an invitation, I'll think about it." I wish I could *stop* thinking about it.

"Call us back when you're free. Your dad texted that he saw some new bird this morning, and we all know you'll appreciate that story more than I will."

It was a cerulean warbler. Earlier this morning, Dad sent me a blurry picture of a tree branch, along with a string of barely coherent texts littered with f-bombs. I know better than to call him when he's bird-watching. He doesn't like to talk much in the first place, but especially not when it might scare the birds away. Still, I'm sure he'd love to debrief about it with someone who understands the excitement of seeing a new species. Especially a bird that's hard to spot, and whose old-growth deciduous canopy habitat is in decline thanks to Minnesota's history of over-harvesting timber—

A *dingdong "doors closing"* from the train station reminds me I'm trying to get Mom off the phone. "Yeah, I'll call when I can."

"You're so busy! I'm so proud of you! My babygi—adult person, a lawyer! You're gonna save the world from climate change one day!" Step three: the shower of love—the longest part of her goodbye if I let her keep going. At least she's getting better about the gendered pet names in this part.

"Thanks, Mom." I'm not busy, nor will I save the world from climate change. I mean, I *keep* busy, buried in books and case studies. Exams are next week, marking the unofficial completion of my Juris Doctorate. The bigger time suck has been studying for the bar exam in July, after which I start as an associate attorney at the environmental law firm where I did an internship last year. I won't be hired officially until I get my results, so I can't afford to slack off.

What matters is passing the bar, not the degree. That's the end goal. That's when I can start my life again. Until then, I can't afford distractions. These monthly brunches are the only social activity I've allowed myself since moving here.

Mom makes that hum again, and I panic for a second that she's going to say something else, but it's just the final step of our goodbye. "I miss you, and I love you, and I hope you have a wonderful day!"

"Love you too." I make myself smile for her sake. "Say hi to Dad for me."

Mom makes kissy noises until I finally hang up. I love her, but I'm definitely my father's kid. Luckily, she doesn't take our lack of enthusiastic affection personally. She knows I'm more reserved, albeit not as much as Dad. His excitement for birds is far more exuberant than his love for us, even as devoted as he is. We all meet each other halfway.

My tiny, cluttered studio feels enormous without Mom's voice coming through the phone. The quiet aches; I can never fill a space the way she so effortlessly does. Mom is a lot, and not always everything I need, but I miss her and Dad and home and Matt and Allie more than I could ever have imagined.

Which makes the charming pink envelope on the coffee table all the more jarring, a siren song beckoning me back to a life that's no longer mine.

I should get ready to leave. If I'm too late to brunch, I'm gonna get stuck sitting next to Eris, instead of someone capable of pleasant conversation, and I'd rather enjoy my only social excursion for the month. I should get up, change into something cooler and gayer than my tank top and joggers, and not think about this damn wedding.

But what if Mom was right? What if this invite is sincere, and not a gesture of disingenuous pity, like I assumed when it arrived four months after everyone else's? What if Matt's parents (or, more likely, Allie's bitchy sister) quietly removed my invite from the stack?

Matt and Allie both still text daily in the group chat that's just the three of us. Ever since the wedding invites went out to everyone but me, I've only responded when they ask me something directly.

That they announced their engagement via group text after the holidays, a mere week after I returned to Chicago, was painful enough. I tried not to take it personally; they're conflict avoidant, like me. I rationalized it as them giving me room to process the news in private. But not even getting an invitation? That cut deep. What else could I do, when they apparently didn't want me in their life anymore? I pulled away.

If Matt and Allie thought they already sent an invitation, what have they thought about me these past four months? Do they think I'm pulling away from them because I'm upset? Because I don't want them to get married? Because I don't love them anymore?

With a heavy sigh, I pick up the envelope, tearing an ugly gash through the pretty, perfect, pink paper.

Two

BRUNCH

Putting my ID away, I scan the crowd for Adrienne. Tucked away in a courtyard behind the bar, the buzzing patio is bright with late-morning sun. The scar tissue in my bum knee aches, I'm hot, and I can't quite catch my breath after walking so fast in a binder. Or perhaps the anxiety sitting heavy in my chest, made worse by the sinking dread that I'm late to brunch, is what's really restricting my breathing.

Both the pain and the panic are my own damn fault. After opening the envelope, I spiraled, staring into the middle distance for far too long, then practically ran here after throwing on jeans and a plain black t-shirt (neither cool nor particularly gay). Being late was inevitable; I shouldn't have rushed.

Spotting Adrienne's shiny scalp on the far side of the patio, I curse myself for opening the damn envelope. I'm technically early; the show always starts fifteen minutes late. But I'm late enough that there's only one open seat left at the table.

Right across from Eris fucking Garcia.

It shouldn't matter. It's only a few minutes of painfully awkward small talk with the only weirdo I don't click with. We're outside, and there are only six of us; I could sit quietly and listen to Dream, the resident extrovert, talk. But Eris is like an accident on the freeway that I can't keep from rubbernecking as I pass.

I linger at the edge of the patio, squinting in the sunlight, peeking under the umbrellas that never provide enough shade. The temptation to say I didn't see them is strong. Then I could run home and finish my existential crisis in peace. Or better yet, bury it in case studies. That's worked well enough the last two years.

But Adrienne spots me first. "Blake!" She waves an unfairly buff arm, gold bangles gleaming against her deep ebony skin. "Over here!"

I wave back, forcing a smile as I make my way to the table. "Hey everyone!"

"Everyone" consists of one extrovert, Dream, and the five shut-ins she's collected. The first is Dream's wife, Adrienne, my friend from law school who immediately clocked me as a fellow queer and sat by me in every class. She claims to have social anxiety, but she's more my security blanket than I am hers. If I hadn't been heartbroken when we met, and she hadn't immediately dropped a "my wife" into the conversation, I probably would have fallen for her real quick. She's buff as hell, shaves her head to the scalp, wears a lot of pretty jewelry, and always has on these high-neck tank tops that make her shoulders look massive. She's all-around gorgeous.

I would never have had a chance, because Dream is the most glamorous femme I've ever laid eyes on. I don't know what perfume she wears, but she always smells amazing. Her thick brown hair is styled in a bob so sharp it could cut someone, and her social media is perfectly curated. For work, she does cosmetic tattoos, somehow making the swollen bold eyebrows, reconstructed fake nipples, and bloody lips she just finished tattooing look perfect.

The other two shut-ins—Stella and Kelsey—I don't know as well. I'm not sure where Dream found them, but they're cool, I guess. Stella is quiet, but they say really profound shit on the rare occasion they do talk. Kelsey's blunt eagerness to devour drama and gossip reminds me of Allie's bitchy twin sister, so I haven't really gotten to know her; small talk fills our silences.

Unlike the other shut-in Dream has collected, Eris, who greets me with a "Sup" when I sit down across from zim. Ze seems incapable of polite conversation.

"Hey." I eagerly grab the mimosa pitcher Adrienne passes me, filling my empty flute. The cheap champagne with a spritz of orange juice is a relief, washing down the anxiety building like bile in my throat.

Really, Eris is a perfectly... Well, not average, or normal, or any other polite descriptors. Eris is Dream's former coworker at the tattoo studio, until ze got a job at a dispensary instead. I think what bothers me most about Eris is that I don't like zim. Because I work very hard at being nice to everyone, and I especially want to befriend the few non-binary and genderqueer people I know.

But Eris is a dick, and I can't stand zim, because I always want to be a dick right back, and I can't. Because then everyone will know I'm not actually that nice, and I'll lose the only friends I have.

The second time we met, I asked, very politely and purely out of curiosity, why ze uses ze/zim/zis pronouns. Eris must have taken it as a criticism, because ze told me to mind my own fucking business. With all of these potential new friends looking at me, waiting for my reaction—just like everyone back in Solberg, desperate for something to gossip about—I swallowed all of my retorts and muttered a "sorry" instead.

Since then, I've minded my own fucking business when it comes to Eris, but our rapport has not improved in the least. Ze gets under my skin no matter how hard I try to be polite, and I hate it. Eris must see through my nice facade because ze works relentlessly to bring out all the bitchy replies in my mind, like ze's determined to break me.

The part of me that sees the best in people recognizes that Eris is probably attractive. Ze is just as buff as Adrienne—if shorter, thicker, and hairier—with lots of piercings and tattoos. Like many tattoo artists, who practice on each other and themselves, most of Eris's are either poorly done or just strange. Such as the rose in the crook of zis elbow, which is actually a poorly-disguised vulva. In addition to big brown eyes with unfairly long lashes, ze has nice hair, long and thick and a lovely chestnut brown color. On the rare occasions when zis undercut is fresh, the geometric patterns tattooed into zis scalp blend into the fade.

I'll grant that Eris is interesting to look at, but ze is just unkempt enough that it bothers me. Not that I'm particularly kempt, but I don't want to like zim, so I focus on the faults. Little imperfections draw my eye: two divots below zis lip where ze used to have snakebite piercings, a scar interrupting zis eyebrow when the barbell got yanked out, the wisps of mustache curling over zis lip in desperate need of a trim. Zis clothes are pretty, but they never quite fit well. A lot of florals, beads, and lace, paired with leather accessories. Like if a grandma was a biker.

"The fuck you lookin' at?" Eris asks, because I'm glaring at zim as I chug my mimosa.

Cheeks burning, I pant as I empty the glass and immediately refill it. I mutter a, "Nothing, sorry," instead of any of the snappy comebacks I'll come up with when I replay this conversation again and again over the next few days.

"You okay there, Blake?" Dream asks, an amused smile on her face.

"Never better," I smile, but based on everyone's concerned looks, I'm grimacing.

Well, mostly concerned; Kelsey practically lights up. "What's wrong?"

I wave her off. "Nothing! How's everyone else?"

"Don't do that, babe," Dream reaches across the table to pat my hand. "You look like someone put chili powder in your panties. Let it out."

"How about I keep it in?" I mutter into my mimosa, hoping it sounds like a joke. But only Eris laughs, which adds insult to injury.

I shouldn't have opened that damn envelope.

It was supposed to be easy. Impersonal. They were supposed to be dotting their I's and crossing their T's, would be secretly relieved when I declined their invitation.

But no. Allie had to include a damn handwritten note in her annoyingly legible script. A heartfelt, personalized missive about how she should have mailed the invitations herself, instead of letting Jessica, her bitchy (my word, not hers) twin sister and maid of honor, do it. How it would mean the world for me to attend, so much so that they already booked a hotel room for me. How both she and Matt have been overthinking if they should have talked to me after I didn't respond to the invite. That they really hope I come, and I should invite the person I'm seeing to come as a plus-one. Even if it's not serious, they want to get to know whoever is in my life, because I never talk about myself enough, and they want to know what my life is like now from an outside source. Because they love me and miss me and want to stay involved in my life. And I'm always welcome in theirs.

So now I *have* to go to the damn wedding. But Matt, Allie, all of their friends, and his parents, they all expect me to be someone I'm not. Matt's parents expect the worst of me, and I can't let them win on principle, so I have to go out of spite. They expected me to come crawling back to Solberg with my tail between my legs, that pursuing a JD was a waste of time. Just like they thought Matt going to college was a waste, so he didn't. But even if Matt always bent to their pressure, I refuse to let the Jacobsons dictate my future. Partially why they never liked me.

Matt's friends, all of whom are heteronormatively coupled up, expect me to move on, leave Matt and Allie alone, and have no feelings but distant happiness for them. As if my life hasn't been entwined with Matt's for our whole lives, as if Allie and I didn't live together for four years. Because I *am* happy for Matt and Allie, though I'm also hurt and jealous. I should be more over it than I am after almost two years, but I'm not.

I'm better off in Chicago than trapped in Solberg. Matt's happier with Allie. She's happy with him; the small town that stifled me provides solace for her. She never could have built a life with us, because Matt never wanted an "us" that was all three of us, and Allie never wanted me. I get it. I have other feelings besides acceptance and compersion. But that doesn't mean I can't be happy for them. They're still my best friends.

Most importantly, Matt and Allie think I'm happy. That I'm living my best life, thriving in the big city, and spreading my gay little wings. All of the things Matt said I needed to do when he broke up with me. Because that's what I've told them.

Yeah, I'm going on dates. Yeah, I'm seeing someone, but I'm not sure if it's going to work out yet, so I don't want to share too much. Yeah, I have a ton of friends, we go to drag brunch all the time! Yeah, my apartment is great, too bad it's so small, otherwise I'd invite you to visit. Yeah, classes are amazing! Yeah, I'm confident I'm going to pass the bar on the first try.

But I'm not doing any of those things, unless this pity invite to drag brunch counts as having friends. No, I'm having an existential crisis and chugging a mimosa, sitting across from a dickhead currently flicking me off. Because, for the second time in five minutes, I'm glaring at zim while chugging a mimosa.

Dream swats Eris's hand away. "Bitch, be nice. Blake is obviously going through something."

"Can they go through something without making that stank-ass face at me?" Eris flicks me off with zis other hand, holding it out so Dream can't reach.

"Sorry." I screw my eyes shut because that's easier than smiling at zim.

Eris has the audacity to laugh. Zis laugh gets on my nerves, too. It's a high-pitched cackle, which is weird considering how deep and gravelly zis voice is.

"Come on, Blake, spill," Adrienne teases, rubbing my shoulder. "If you don't tell us here, I'm going to ask you before class, and you'll have uptight law students eavesdropping on your drama, instead of tipsy, supportive queers."

I groan. "My best friends are getting married. To each other."

"We already knew that. You told us months ago," says Kelsey. "One of them is your ex you were with for eight years. They got together suspiciously quick, didn't even warn you that they were getting engaged before texting it to your group chat, and then they didn't invite you."

Kelsey creeps me out a little. I don't know anything about her, not even her last name. I suppose that's on me for not being the best listener in group conversations. It all blends together until someone speaks to me directly.

I sigh, knowing that between Dream and Kelsey, they're going to get the explanation out of me anyway, so I'll stick to the facts; they can jump to conclusions about any too-vulnerable feelings. "Turns out they meant to invite me, but the maid of honor 'lost' my invite, and they just found out, and they were really apologetic and hope I still come."

"Why not go, then?" Dream asks, like the extrovert she is. "Like yeah, you're the ex and shit, but like, you're queer. We do exes differently."

"They're all straight, though," Adrienne reminds her. "The bride and groom might be Blake's friend, but for everyone else at the wedding, exes don't get invites. They'll be an outsider amongst the people who are basically their ex-future in-laws."

"Gross," Eris and I say together, scowling at each other.

"I didn't want them to be my future in-laws," I explain. "That's part of the awkwardness with going. They wanted a daughter-in-law who was easy to push around."

"Are you not easy to push around?" Eris asks skeptically. "You're a doormat."

"Thanks, Eris." I shake my head, hating how Eris not only sees the parts of me I don't want to acknowledge, but announces them for everyone to hear. "But I do have a spine, and that spine didn't fit back in the closet once I came out. So no, I'm not as easy to push around as Matt's parents wanted. Namely, I wouldn't be a *daughter*-in-law, and I never let them forget that."

Correcting the Jacobsons when they misgendered me was easier than my own parents. Probably because I want my parents to like me, and that was a lost cause with the Jacobsons. They don't even like Matt, and he's their son. But they like Allie, and that says a lot about Allie's lack of spine. God, everyone is probably walking all over her. No wonder the invites were pink. She *hates* pink.

"Again, so why not go?" Dream asks. "You don't need to make nice with his parents. You have friends to hang out with."

I don't, but I don't want to admit that. "Everyone I used to be friends with is married or engaged, and I'd be the only queer person *and* the only single person." I sigh, adding in a mutter, "And I kinda hinted I was seeing someone, and they want me to bring them as a plus-one."

"What?" Kelsey asks. "You got quiet."

"They lied about how single they are, and now everyone expects them to show up to the wedding with a hot piece of ass," Eris supplies.

I glare at zim, but ze only smirks.

"Oh my god," Kelsey squeals. "This is amazing! You should totally hire an actor off Craigslist to play your fake lover, and see how far you can take it before they figure out you're not actually together."

The table turns to look at her with shared incredulity.

"Are you trying to get them killed?" Adrienne asks. "Blake, do not do that."

"Wasn't gonna," I deadpan. "Sounds expensive."

Eris snorts.

"Why did you lie?" Dream asks.

I chug another mimosa, hoping the conversation will shift to literally anything or anyone else. But no, they're all enraptured by my misfortune. Even Eris, who chugs zis own mimosa while meeting my glare this time. I muffle a belch before answering, "Because I wanted them to think I was happy."

"Can you not be happy *and* single? You're in law school!" Adrienne scoffs. "I do not envy anyone trying to date in grad school. Thank goodness I'm already married." She and Dream exchange a flirty look.

"Yeah, of course." I could be happy being single, in theory. But I refuse to admit that I'm not happy in front of the only friends I have. "But I had to be happy enough so Matt could allow himself to be happy too. And that meant acting like I'd moved on, so he could move on."

"To Allie," Kelsey says.

I nod. I knew it was coming. Hell, I *wanted* it to happen. I just didn't expect it to happen so *quick*. When I was still in the picture, Matt and Allie platonically loved each other something fierce, and the lines between friendship and love for Matt have always been thin. Allie trusted Matt to have her back, since she so rarely had her own. It was inevitable, and I wanted them to—

"I'll do it," comes that less-grating-than-it-should-be voice from across the table.

I frown at Eris. "Do what?"

"Be your fake hot piece of ass for the wedding," ze says, like it's not the most ridiculous idea that has ever left zis mouth.

My face steels into an impassive half smile. I do not want to offend Eris. But no one would ever believe that I'd be into zim. "Uh...I don't think that'll work."

"Why not? I know I'm way cooler than you, but you're not *that* bad-looking," ze says.

I can't tell if ze's teasing, but no one laughs.

Dream smacks zim. "Be nice, fuckface!"

So Eris wasn't teasing. Great. Good to know I'm not just a nerd, I'm an ugly nerd.

"I was just kidding, chill out!" Eris rubs zis arm. "Yeah, Blake's all right or whatever, if you're into that deer in the headlights look. I just thought it'd be fun to crash a wedding and fuck with a bunch of uptight white people. I assume everyone's white, right?" ze asks me.

I nod. "Pretty much."

"And like, not KKK white, or call-ICE-even-though-I'm-from-Texas white, right?" Eris asks, that marred eyebrow raised into a point. "That would make this plan significantly less fun."

"No!" I pause, mentally running through the members of Allie's extended family. "Yeah, no. There's some religious people, but they usually ignore my existence."

"Sweet. Let's fucking go, bro!" Eris extends zis fist expectantly across the table.

"You're just not..." Staring blankly at the "odio" tattooed across zis knuckles, I gape, searching for an explanation that won't make me sound like a horrible person. But no, as far as Eris is concerned, I'm an ugly nerd *and* an asshole; I might as well embrace it. If I can be myself around anyone, it's Eris. "You're not exactly who I'd bring home to convince people that I'm doing okay."

Eris drops zis fist, and for a split second, I hate that I've disappointed zim. But Eris just claps, letting out that high-pitched cackle. "Exactly. We can confuse them!"

I blink, confused myself.

"This is your chance to fuck with the uptight people who want you to be small and quiet. Bringing home a short, hairy, chubby genderfuck weirdo and acting like you traded up from your golden boy next door is going to fuck with their minds, dude! And if your best friends are really your friends, they'll be happy you're happy, so don't worry about them." Eris gestures for my phone. "Let me give you my number. Text me the deets, and you can have some fun lying to the people you let walk all over you."

"I don't let them walk all over me." For some reason I can't explain beyond sheer desperation, I pass zim my phone.

Eris raises zis eyebrow with the scar, stark white against zis tan skin and the dark brown of zis thick brows. "You barely put up a fight against *me* just now, and you don't even like me."

A tiny intake of breath comes from the otherwise silent Stella, a sign that they have gathered their courage. We all turn to them, waiting. I'm relieved I don't have to pretend to like Eris for the sake of propriety.

"Happiness isn't found in other people," Stella says, their thin voice wavering. Their deep brown eyes are thoughtful as they look at me and Eris in turn. "It's created by appreciating the beauty in front of you."

For some reason, everyone but Eris and I laugh. Eris chucks a crumpled-up napkin at Stella, who bats it away, still wearing a shy smile. I roll my eyes. Honestly, that's too far even for Eris, made especially rude considering how rarely Stella talks.

But before I can call zim out on zis bullshit, the show starts. The speakers blasting "We Found Love" by Rihanna drowns out anything else the sage Stella might have mustered.

Three

BAMBI

Sprawled on the couch in my small, messy shithole of an apartment, I accept that I'm too tipsy to study. Chugging that many mimosas was very shortsighted; not only is my mouth sticky from maple syrup and cheap champagne, but my afternoon study block is wasted. Just like me. Whose genius idea was it to study after brunch, anyway?

In a rare break from the carefully planned study schedule that lets me feel in control of my loneliness, I don't open my laptop. Instead, I grab my phone, ignoring the new messages from my parents, Matt, and Allie—all asking if I got the invite. With how much my head is spinning, I'd probably say some impulsive shit and find myself in a worse situation than I'm already in. I'll respond to those when I'm sober. Once I've figured out what I want to do.

Talking it out over brunch made it clear that I *want* to go to the wedding. I want to see Matt and Allie cute and happy. I want their friends who think I should disappear quietly to know I can be in their life. Just in a new, uncomfortable, but still loving way. And (this is very unkind of me) I really want to see Matt's parents and Allie's bitchy sister eat shit when I show up.

But preferably not with Eris, so I open one of the dating apps I frequent. And by frequent, I mean look at profiles, perhaps match with someone who seems nice, then never reply to their messages. Because Adrienne was right; finding time to date in law school is hard. But also, I've never dated. Never expected I'd have to learn. So I have no idea what I'm doing.

Matt and I just happened. Since preschool, we were best friends and constant companions. Then, the summer before we started high school, I got hit by a truck. After that, everything was different between us. We'd been crushing on each other since puberty erupted, unsure what to do with the confusing feelings and urges, but a near-death experience really amped up the hormones. Neither of us cared to pretend we weren't each other's person after I almost died. We were each other's first kiss in my hospital bed, and by the time I was discharged a month later, more than one nurse had walked in on us making out.

Dating apps are all so intimidating in comparison. Swiping through the hot single queers in my area, I read profile after profile, ferreting out excuses why it wouldn't work. Finding a fake date is no less terrifying than a real one. I'm sure it requires me to message someone, but what do I say? How do I know that I can trust them enough to drive six hours to a small-ass town, two states away? Or convince them to trust me? What if they're annoying, and I have to be fake around *them* the whole weekend too?

I groan, dreading going back already, even if I love home. Being so nice and polite and considerate all the time is exhausting. Everyone in Solberg has known me since my mom was hired at Sigurdsson College when I was two, and townies thrive on gossip. If I ever slipped up and let the sarcasm out with the wrong person, or even burped without pretending to be ashamed of my bodily functions, it reflected on my parents. My wonderful, strange parents who are already the weirdos in Solberg. Growing up, I had to be as normal as humanly possible, so things wouldn't be harder on my spitfire, opinionated mother and my awkward, disabled father.

My chest hurts just thinking about it, my binder growing too tight. My skin crawls, like it might burst open. I can't move back. Living in the city means that I don't have to care what people think all the goddamn time. I'm free here. Free to not smile at everyone. Free to do the bare minimum. Free to disappear and be alone, even when I'm surrounded by people. I don't have to constantly contain myself to fit in like I did in Solberg. There, I was only ever truly free with Matt and Allie.

In the midst of my mindless swipes left, a new text makes my phone vibrate.

> So we doin this or nah?

I sigh, wondering how Eris got my number. Then I see ze texted zimself a middle finger emoji when adding zis number to my phone.

With a groan, I sit up, my bum knee protesting after speedwalking from the Red Line earlier in my rush to get to brunch. Are we doing this? I could just tell Matt and Allie that I love them, but it's better I don't go, like my parents did. Or I could tell them that I'm actually single, go to the wedding, and be the awkward third-wheel around Matt's friends.

> You can say no. I know that word confuses you.

I huff. Eris has a point, I'm not good at saying no. But if I can say no to anyone, it's zim. Eris sees the judgmental asshole behind the airs I put on to convince Adrienne and Dream that I'm a good person, in hopes that we'll be friends for real one day. Ze always makes me feel so...exposed. I hate it.

> I have no qualms about saying no. Especially to you.

> So...yes, then? Imma be your hot piece of ass for your ex's wedding?

I wince. Maybe I drank too much at brunch; my stomach is not settling well at the prospect of driving the six hours to Solberg, trapped in a car with Eris. I rub my sternum, willing it to stop fluttering and let me breathe.

After the long car ride on Friday, the schedule will include a rehearsal dinner full of fake-nice small talk. I would need to hold hands with Eris or some shit to be convincing. Ze probably has sweaty palms. Does Eris even have a fake side, or would ze be a sarcastic shithead the whole time? A snort escapes me as I imagine how Mr. and Mrs. Jacobson might react to seeing me there in the first place, let alone with someone like Eris. Ze doesn't fit into their sanitized, orderly view of the world.

We'd have to spend a night in the hotel together. The champagne buzz under my skin makes me uncomfortably warm. Whatever, it's only a big deal if Eris snores. Which ze probably does. I'm sure we'd spend the night ignoring each other anyway.

The morning of the wedding, we could ignore each other more before heading to campus in the late afternoon. While Matt's parents frown upon higher education (likely on account of their long-standing feud with my professor mother), Allie's parents went to Siggurdson too, and all Siggys get married on campus. I was already wary of marriage, but four years of the constant heteronormative "Siggys marry Siggys!" and "Ring by spring!" bullshit has turned me off to the institution completely.

For myself, anyway. Matt and Allie's will be cute.

After the wedding is the reception—which I expect will be more fun than the rehearsal dinner on account of the DJ and the open bar—followed by one more night of Eris and I ignoring each other in the hotel. The six-hour drive back will be silent, I'm sure. I hope.

I deeply appreciate the fact that my parents will be out of town. This way, they can't insist on meeting Eris until after the wedding. I can tell everyone we've broken up before it comes to that—

I groan. "Ugh, we're fucking doing this aren't we?"

If nothing else, I wouldn't have to fake anything with zim, like I would with literally everyone else. Maybe the quality time will help me find something redeemable in Eris. Or be the excuse to skip brunch forever.

If I say yes, can you promise not to be a complete asshole? It's a small town, so everything we do will get back to my parents, and they're already going to be hurt that I'm bringing someone home when they're out of town.

You're lying to your parents too? That's cold, Bambi!

Whatever, they're happier with the partial truths I give them. And Matt still helps out my parents constantly, so he's probably told them I'm seeing someone. Explains why my mom keeps fishing for clues about my social life. She doesn't push, which I appreciate, but I have no shame in letting them believe whatever makes them more comfortable— Wait, the fuck did ze call me?

The fuck? Bambi?

I figure we should have cute pet names. And you always look like a baby deer staring down a semitruck on the freeway whenever I say anything to you.

My stomach lurches at the memory of literally staring down a truck on a highway, but I haven't told anyone in Chicago about that, and I'm not going to start with Eris. Everyone in Solberg was so...careful with me. Patronizing, even after I no longer needed a wheelchair. So "nice" that

I could never assert myself for fear of offending someone. Eris is already aggravating enough without treating me with kid gloves.

What are you gonna call me?

Nothing.

Awww come on, Bambi, is that any way to treat your hot piece of ass?

Stop saying that! Can you or can you not contain your assholery for one weekend? I need us to not reflect poorly on my parents.

Make me.

Are we sharing your childhood bed for the weekend? ;)

No, we have a hotel. Hopefully, it has two beds, but Allie booked it, so you might need to sleep on the floor.

Again, make me.

When can we hang out?

> Why would we hang out?

You gotta make it convincing. We gotta talk logistics, make a plan, do our hard launch, tell me how to handle the ex and shit. You really haven't thought through this plan at all, have you?

> I still haven't decided if it's happening. WTF is a hard launch...?

Are your friends gonna believe that it's serious enough for me to attend your ex's wedding if we literally have no pictures together on social media? Hell no, so we gotta announce our relationship now, so they believe your lies!

> Dream takes pictures of us at brunch.

You're so hardheaded, Bambi. Those are group pictures. It's not the same.

> Is this what you're like with people you're actually dating? Coercing them into hanging out with you?

> No, I never have to try this hard. They're usually begging for alone time with me. ;)

I'm not really sure how to react to that, so I stick to Eris's original question.

> I have finals this week, so anytime after Friday morning.

> Come by the dispensary at 2. We'll celebrate with ice cream.

> Fine.

> It's a date!

> It's not a date. It's merely logistics planning.

> You're killing me, Bambi.

> Good.

> lmaoooooooo

Four

Bud

The L squeals overhead while I walk as self-assuredly as my knee allows, checking my phone to make sure I went the right direction from the platform.

I didn't.

With an audible groan, I pretend I forgot something and head in the opposite direction, even though I'm sure no one is looking at me. Two years in this city, and I still get lost everywhere I go. Chicago feels surreal for someone who grew up in a town of two thousand people. Well four, counting the college students.

A mere hour ago, I completed the last of my exams. For all intents and purposes, I now have a law degree. It hasn't quite sunk in yet, and I'm not sure I'll notice when it does.

There's something odd about a phase of life that's over, but hasn't yet ended. There's not a Before and After. It's like on a hike, when one biome changes to another. Sometimes, it's sudden and noticeable, like when a body of water disrupts the gradation. That was the end of my time in Solberg. I graduated, questioning my decision to move away for law school. A few days later, Matt broke up with me, and I fled, moving here three months ahead of schedule. It was a clean cut. No liminal blend between phases. I blinked and found myself staring out across Lake Michigan instead of farm fields.

Other times, the transition is slow. The patches of sunlight that filter through the forest canopy grow bigger and more frequent, until only a few oak trees dot the prairie. That's how I feel right now.

For the last two years of my life, I've been focused solely on passing tests and writing papers, much like all of my schooling before. But now, there's no next degree to work towards. I'm in that in-between space, where clusters of trees ease into prairie, because I still have to study full-time until I take the bar in six weeks. Part of me wants to go back to the forest; the dense canopy makes me feel safe. But the whole point of going on the hike was to see the prairie. So of course I'll keep on the path, even if I feel more exposed and vulnerable with every sun-dappled step towards that vast openness of the Rest of My Life.

A loud honk makes me flinch, body bracing for impact, though the van is across the street. The second I've exhaled my panic, someone shouts, seemingly directed at me, and I tense again. But I keep walking the way Adrienne taught me, though every fiber of my upbringing fights against ignoring someone yelling. In Solberg, there's no ignoring people ever, especially when they're trying to get your attention. But a chaotic melody of arguing and distant honking breaks through my anxiety. I scold myself for being egotistical; that shout was never meant for me. I'm no one here, and I love that.

I really underestimated what life in a city would be like. I visited the campus with my mom, who's originally from Boston and travels a lot for academic conferences. She knew how to get around, and I just followed her. Luckily, Adrienne grew up here; she helped me get used to it. *"If you don't want to get shouted at, don't stop and let them shout at you. Just keep moving, and pay them no mind. Keep an eye out for anyone following you, but whatever everyone else does is none of your business."* I appreciate that. Minding my own business would have been incredibly rude in Solberg.

I reach the dispensary where Eris works without incident. The cacophony of the city disappears in this quiet room, the sunlight dimmed by dozens of plants. Spacey new age ambient music plays on hidden speakers, and the air is thick and dank, despite the no-smoking sign on the wall.

"Sup," the person behind the counter greets me when I walk in, sounding so eerily like Eris that I'm surprised it's not zim. But this person is tall and thin, bald with a massive beard, wearing a polo with a cartoon cannabis flower embroidered on the chest and a he/him button on his lanyard.

"Hi, I'm looking for Eris?" My voice sounds so timid I want to cringe. I grip my backpack tighter.

"Blake Ryan?" The guy asks, tapping the counter in an idle rhythm.

I nod, wondering what the fuck Eris told him that warranted sharing my last name, because this man's glower is slightly terrifying. But he eventually grins, and I relax a little. "You're taller *and* prettier than I expected. Eris normally doesn't have good taste."

My stomach clenches; I hate being called pretty. Still, I stammer out, "Thank you?"

"Hey!" Eris's muscled, tattooed arm pokes through some plastic sheeting covering a doorway. Clad in a latex glove—though the scriptwork "And I Say Fuck It" tattooed on zis forearm is still visible—zis hand flicks off the guy behind the counter. "Shut the fuck up." The disembodied hand then points at me. "Come here! Don't listen to any of his bullshit."

The guy laughs as I duck through the plastic sheeting, behind which Eris's arm has already disappeared. My jaw clenches. I'm voluntarily spending a weekend in my hometown with this person? As the plastic falls behind me, Eris is fussing around a small grow room. Cannabis plants in different stages of growth line the metal tables under the bright lights.

"Put this on." Eris hands me a hairnet and latex gloves. Ze is much shorter than I expect in tennis shoes, instead of the platform boots ze wears to brunch. I've never seen Eris in a polo before, or with zis hair pulled back into a bun either. This doesn't look like the Eris I know. It's weird.

I put the hairnet on, tucking in the longer curls at my neck. "I didn't think dispensaries could grow it on-site."

"You can't. These are for breeding, not selling." Ze hands me a face mask and slips a pair of safety glasses onto my face. I glare at zim but stay still while ze works the arms over my ears. Eris gives me a smug grin. "You're early, so you're gonna make yourself useful, while I make these plants fuck."

"You're such a delight."

"I know." Ze hands me a large bin with a half-wilted cut plant and a tiny pair of scissors inside. "Cut the fan and sugar leaves off, but be careful with the buds." Ze points to the smaller leaves curling around the sticky flowers.

I'm slightly offended that ze thinks I don't know my way around a cannabis plant; my parent's basement is far more impressive than this room. "I was promised ice cream, not manual labor." But me being me, I pick up the scissors and start with the larger fan leaves, stacking them in a neat pile in the corner of the bin. The grassy smell is pleasant, like fresh citrus.

"I told you two. It's only one."

I shrug. "I finished my last exam early."

"Wait, you *just* finished exams?" Eris asks, looking over zis shoulder as ze prods a plant with a cotton swab.

"Yeah. That's what I said in my text." I don't know what's confusing.

"Why aren't you out celebrating, bro?" ze asks, turning back to the plant.

"I'm celebrating by not studying for the bar today." I pause, squinting so I don't nip a bud when I snip a sugar leaf. "And I *thought* ice cream. But apparently, I'm getting roped into your shady weed operation instead."

Eris laughs. "It's not shady. I'm contracted by the state to breed hybrid strains for research purposes."

I frown. "Aren't you the retail manager?"

Ze nods. "Yeah, and the owner sublets the grow room to me as a lab. Until he can grow here legally, he figures we might as well get paid by the government, instead of letting the space go to waste."

I rack my exhausted brain; something isn't adding up. "You were a tattoo artist a year ago."

Eris snorts. "I'm honestly impressed you remember that. You don't pay attention to shit."

"I pay attention!"

"Tell me literally anything about Kelsey." Eris looks over zis shoulder at me with a shit-eating grin.

I grumble under my breath, too tired to pretend to be a decent person. Eris already knows I'm not. "She's...got a good memory."

Ze lets out a full-on cackle this time, with the high pitch and everything. "Exactly. You don't listen for shit. But I don't talk much, so you didn't know anything about my shady weed operation."

"You talk *too* much," I retort. It's still not clicking for me, from a legal perspective. Why would the government hire a random dispensary employee to grow their experimental strains? "For the purpose of telling my parents, how did you get into this?"

Ze smirks. "In case your *parents* are curious, I have a masters in agricultural science and lab management experience. Unclench, Bambi, it's all legal."

The nickname sounds different in zis gravelly voice. The hint of a Texas accent softens the consonants, night and day from the strong Minnesota vowels in my mind when I'd read it. I swallow. "Then why were you a tattoo artist?"

"I wanted to be." Eris shrugs and moves zis collection of cotton swabs to another plant, unzipping the humidity tent around it. "And then I wanted to do this."

"That's an unsatisfying answer."

As a response, Eris merely hums in amusement.

We finish our work in silence. Peeling the PPE off, I wait impatiently while Eris cleans up. With zis hands on my shoulders, Eris hurries me out past the guy in the lobby, telling him to shut the fuck up. Before he can say anything, I'm rushed out the door.

I turn around to chew zim out for being pushy, but Eris is already zipping down the sidewalk. For someone four inches shorter than me, ze walks fast. I push myself to keep up, following half a pace behind. I can't hide my limp walking this fast, and I don't want Eris to notice. No one here constantly fusses over me the way Matt and my parents did, and I don't want that to start now. I appreciate that Eris treats me just as rudely as everyone else. "Where are we going?"

"Ice cream."

"Oh, okay, because that clears it up."

Ze huffs. "There's a cute spot by the river that has vegan ice cream."

"You're not vegan." Eris always gets bacon with brunch.

"No, but you're lactose intolerant."

I sputter, my brow knitting in confusion. "How the fuck do you know that?"

"Because my brain isn't stuffed full of boring law shit, so I can pay attention to my surroundings." Eris looks over zis shoulder, pushing me to the side just as a bike zips past. My hair tickles my cheek; if I'd stayed a few inches to the right, more than just my knee would be hurting right now. "Seriously, it's a miracle you've survived this long."

"Came close," I mutter, breathing through the knot in my gut, as Eris zips along the sidewalk again. I practically have to jog to keep up. Already, I'm dreading how much my knee will hurt later.

By the time I sit on a bench overlooking the river, mint chip cone in hand, my knee crackles like sand is caught in the joint. I hope Eris doesn't hear it. Ze doesn't say anything as ze sits, far too close to me, so the sound must have been drowned out amidst the cacophony of the concrete jungle around us.

"Take a picture," ze tells me, dragging zis tongue up the side of the rocky road cone in a way that is frankly obscene.

"You could say please." I take my phone out anyway, mostly to stop myself from staring. "Why can't *you* take a picture?"

Eris sighs with a condescending air. "Bambi, this is our hard launch. We both need to post a few pictures. So go on, take a picture of your..." Ze looks at me expectantly. "What pet name are you giving me since you won't call me your hot piece of ass?"

I grimace. "I'm not really a nickname person."

"What did you call your ex?"

"Matt."

Ze laughs. "No, like, babe or sweetheart. Punkin. Pookie bear?"

I shake my head. "Dude?"

"Oh my god," ze sighs. "You're really *not* a nickname person. Okay, so what am I? Pal? Homie? Buddy?"

I snort, poking the cartoon cannabis logo on zis sleeve. "I could call you Bud."

Eris sighs. "That is the worst pet name ever, but it'll do. Anyway, take a picture." With a smirk, ze drags zis tongue up the side of the melting ice cream again, gesturing to me to take the shot.

I do, but I don't check how it turned out, because I'm pretty sure Eris has a tongue ring that I'd never noticed before, and I will *not* let myself stare. If the picture is shit, it's shit. Eris can look shitty in our fake hard post, tongue ring and all.

"Do you need to take one of me?" I ask, looking determinedly at the river.

"Already did."

I snap my head up. "What? When?"

"You don't pay attention to anything." Eris snorts. "When you were trying the coconut."

I tsk, sounding just like my mother. "I didn't like that flavor."

"I know. Your face was funny. That's why I took a picture."

I groan. "You're such a considerate fake partner, Bud."

"Aww, I like you too, Bambi," ze teases. "Anyway, we should take a couple selfies, too. Give me your phone."

"Why?"

Ze looks at me like I'm being intentionally obtuse. "Because the light is better from my angle? I know you haven't dated in a while, but this is rudimentary stuff. You never took selfies with Matt?"

"Allie always did that. Or Matt would because he was the tallest." I shrug, tasting my ice cream, the mint flavor sharp and sweet with a nutty undertone.

"Here, turn towards me," ze pats my thighs. The unexpected touch makes me jump.

"You're very bossy." I shift so my body twists towards zim, draping my free arm over the back of the bench. It's nice, letting the rude thoughts out without worrying about what anyone might think. I never realized how much of the real me I was swallowing, without Allie and Matt around to let it out.

"And you're a pushover." Passing me zis ice cream cone (my traitorous hand simply takes it), Eris pulls zis polo off, shorting out my brain into static. The light brown skin of zis broad shoulders is covered in lines of ink. Zis muscular arms flex as Eris lets down zis long hair, shaking out the waves. Left in a red satin cami, Eris settles back against my chest before I can grasp what's happening.

My ice cream is frozen midair, halfway to my open mouth.

While my brain fights to process the solid body against mine, Eris snuggles into me. Zis brown hair smells like weed and citrus as it tickles my face. A strong hand grips my forearm to pull it around a warm, hairy, muscular chest covered in satin.

"Bro, you are so stiff right now," Eris teases, zis grip tight on my wrist to lick the rocky road cone still in my hand. "Like, maybe I shoulda warned you. But if you want to convince anyone that you actually like me, maybe get used to physical contact."

"Sorry." The apology escapes my mouth before I can stop it, but I don't know what I'm sorry for. I twist to lick up a drip of mint chip that threatens to run down the side, careful not to let any get in zis hair.

"Don't be. I was lowkey hoping you'd react like this." Eris chuckles.

I swat zis chest before I can think about that, too. But Eris still grips my wrist, so it's not very effective. Especially since I'm still holding zis ice cream.

Ze just laughs, tilting zis chin back against my shoulder to grin at me, far too close to my face. "Perfect. I got a shot of your annoyed scrunchy nose, instead of just the deer in the headlights look."

It's then I remember Eris is taking pictures. I try to scowl, but zis big brown eyes are close enough to count every eyelash. Under such close inspection, the tiny freckles sprinkled across zis nose and cheekbones are revealed to be a colorful spray of tiny star tattoos. The pale divots under Eris's full lips curve as ze smiles.

A boat honks on the river, and I jump. Tearing myself away from the face too close to mine, I watch a tour boat pull up to a dock.

"Relax, Bambi," ze murmurs, low and resonant against my chest. "Just act natural."

I have to fight to keep from squirming, my skin burning. "I'd probably have you in a chokehold, naturally."

"Hot." Eris snorts and settles zis head back against my shoulder, snuggling against my body more firmly. Relaxing against zim in return, I try to mask any reactions, but it's been a very long time since I've cuddled with anyone. Eris's body is solid and warm, and this is...nice. A tiny sigh escapes me. If Eris notices, ze pretends not to. For the sake of pictures to convince Matt and Allie that this is real, I rest my cheek against the smooth brown hair that smells like home and orange peels, and watch the tourists line up to board the boat.

Five

Hard Launch

Numbed by an ice pack, my knee is propped up on a stack of textbooks and a pillow. When I got home a couple of hours ago, I managed to change into my sweatpants, pop some acetaminophen, and get through one round of PT exercises before my knee protested that it was done for today. The Pink Line station outside my apartment is bright enough that I didn't bother getting up to turn on my lights when the sun went down.

Just as the dull ache finally starts to alleviate, my phone buzzes.

The text from Eris is quickly buried by the Instagram notifications that have been blowing up my phone since Eris tagged me in pictures an hour ago. Pictures I haven't even looked at yet. Ze has three thousand followers, as opposed to my hundred and fifty (not many of whom would care if I'm in a relationship, fake or not). This "hard launch" business still seems excessive, and I can't imagine what Eris is getting out of this, besides the cruel satisfaction of annoying me.

Maybe that's the answer.

Bro, why does your IG have they/she for your pronouns? I thought you only used they/them.

I do, but it makes people feel less bad when they mess up. I don't know how to respond when they just keep apologizing.

Jesus fucking Christ, Bambi. I just dented my wall from smashing my forehead into it so hard.

Too bad you didn't knock yourself unconscious.

How are you such a snot with me, and yet the biggest pushover in the world?

I contain multitudes.

I'm done. I'm at my limit with you today.

> That's an option? What did I do so I can do it again?

> Just keep doing what you're doing, which is prioritizing literally everyone other than yourself. It's so fucking annoying.....!

A grin warms my face, and I can't seem to fight it. I should have stopped being nice to Eris ages ago; this is so fun.

While I want to respond that I *do* prioritize myself, ze's not wrong. I care for myself in small ways, ways that don't inconvenience other people, so no one notices and isn't bothered by me. The one time I put myself first was going to law school, and while I don't regret it, that decision created tidal waves.

It's a miracle I came out, honestly. If I hadn't started quite so many conversations with Matt about how hot every celebrity was back in high school, it might have never happened at all. Matt was solidly on team "Only Blake is hot" which I didn't believe then. I thought he was just saying what boyfriends are supposed to say. In comparison, I was a little horndog, even though I'm pretty picky about who I let myself be attracted to.

Now, I believe him, because I'm pretty sure Matt is demisexual. And painfully monogamous—he's only ever had room in his heart for one person, and that person is never going to be a stranger, only his closest friend. When he removed me from his heart, I knew it would soon be filled with Allie instead.

No matter what curveballs I threw at him, Matt always accepted and loved and supported me. I had room in our relationship to prioritize myself. He created space for me to figure myself out, first as bisexual and later as non-binary. He corrected everyone on my pronouns, bought me my first binder, and started calling me his joyfriend instead of girlfriend. Even breaking up with me, when I was starting to doubt if I should move to Chicago, was a decision he made for my own good.

Since trading forests and fields for skyscrapers and traffic, I have nothing but space to put myself first. And yet... If I hadn't gotten ice cream with Eris, and later a drink (because ze had *so* many questions about the wedding and fake-partner logistics), then I would have come home after my exams to smoke a joint instead of studying for the bar, and simply called it a night. So I guess I appreciate that Eris dragged me out to do something sociable instead.

As I'm changing my bio to "they/them," I get a notification about a comment from Adrienne, and curiosity gets the better of me. Her comment reads, "About time this power couple got together!" I have a bunch of follow requests from the rest of the brunch group, so I accept and follow back. Among the comments, there's a "How did you pull this stunner, Eris?" from Dream, and an "Oh my godddd this is happening!!!" followed by a million heart emojis from Kelsey. Stella merely sent a single smirking emoji, to which Eris responded with a row of middle fingers.

Eris told me I didn't have to reply to any comments, but that I should add one on zis post. Wondering what to say, I swipe through the photos. Of course, ze posted the least flattering pictures of me. Me grimacing with the wooden sample spoon in my mouth. My nose scrunched in annoyance while ze eats zis ice cream, a hand with "odio" tattooed on the knuckles wrapped around my wrist. But the last one, me daydreaming and looking out over the water, lips pursed around my ice cream, is kinda artistic, I guess.

After careful consideration, I type, "You're never taking pictures of me again." Eris didn't say I had to leave a *nice* comment, and I don't want to go back to faking nice with zim.

Part of me still wants that celebratory joint, but then I'll get chatty and flirty because Eris showed me an ounce of attention today. Admittedly, I might be a little touch-starved after living on my own for two years, and Eris is a great cuddler. So it's either doomscroll or get high, but not both.

I decide to get high, finding a pre-roll and a lighter amongst the mess on my coffee table.

A flurry of texts from Matt pop up just before I turn it off.

> Duuuudddeeeeeeeeodijtoirgmoir-moirjtgoidrjtgr

> That's who you're bringing to the wedding??????? OH MY GOD!

> This is exactly the type of person I imagined you'd end up dating.

What the fuck is that supposed to mean?

They're so cool!

And that tongue ring with the ice cream? Get it, Bloke! Allie wants to know if I should get one.

I guess he meant it as a compliment? But uff da, that tongue ring indeed! I light the joint to distract myself from *that* train of thought before responding.

Thanks, I think? Ze/zim/zis, btw, not they/them.

Oh, that's gonna be a challenge. I'll start practicing. I can't wait to meet this Eris. Ze seems super cool (Did I use that right?) and you two look so hot together!!! I need to get to know zim(???) better whenever you finally let Allie and I visit you. Which is when, exactly? You still need to send us your graduation deets.

Yes, you got it right, but don't get too excited. Not sure how long this will last.

> Right, sure, because you'd total-ly bring someone you're not crazy about to the wedding.

> Allie said to bring someone even if it wasn't serious.

> Your mom says she wants to meet zim when you're ready.

> ARE YOU WITH THEM RIGHT NOW???

> Yeah. It's Friday Family Game Night.

> I HAVENT TOLD THEM ABOUT ERIS

> lol whoops. You put it online, Blokey!

> On Insta! Not Facebook!

But it's too late. My phone lights up with an incoming video call from my mom. I take a deep drag on the joint to ease the embarrassment and dread before answering. "Hi, Mom."

Her hair fills the screen. "Your young man looks very interesting, Blakey-poo."

"My human person, Mom." Though that's debatable. I choose not to press that passive-aggressive "interesting" she dropped—a Minnesota Nice habit she's picked up in the twenty-four years of living in Solberg. Not that I ever press Mom on anything.

"Oh, he's non-binary too?"

"*Ze*, Linda. *Ze* is non-binary, too," Matt corrects, his tongue buzzing as he drags out the zee sound. I'm tempted to clarify that Eris identifies more closely with genderfuck, but that's technically under the non-binary umbrella. And a deeper dive into gender expression than my parents could handle. "And I, for one, can't wait to see how my parents react when they see just how *interesting* ze is!"

Matt must have taken the phone from my mother, because suddenly I can see all of them. Mom with her henna-dyed red mane of curls; Matt, his strawberry blond mop of hair and freckles popping against his tan skin and gap-toothed beam; Allie, with a sweet smile hiding her shit-eating grin because she's secretly bitchy like me, and we love that about each other; and my dad, his gray hair pulled into his usual ponytail, who waves in the background before going back to squinting at his Scrabble tiles. Must be his turn. Our family takes Scrabble very seriously.

Seeing everyone I love in one place—excited to see me, to be a part of my life, even though I'm not there—hits me hard. Fighting back the burning in my eyes and the yearning ache for a life I can't go back to, I smile, take a hit of the joint, and prepare to be roasted.

Six

GLACIAL MELT

I HATE DRIVING IN the city (part of the reason I never go anywhere), so Eris drives the first leg to the Illinois border. And—because it's a six-hour drive—we're leaving at the ass crack of dawn. As an aspiring lawyer, I should get used to early mornings and navigating rush hour traffic, but I hate getting dressed before nine.

Dressed in my comfiest joggers and t-shirt, I curl up in the passenger seat, a scalding cup of gas station coffee pressed under my nose, snorting the caffeine until it's cool enough to drink. In the driver's seat, Eris talks shit about me. Namely, that I'm eerily quiet without caffeine, what a stereotype I am because I drive an Outback, and the binoculars in the driver's side door, which ze assumes I use while I drive. I choose not to respond because I have, on occasion (in my defense, sandhill cranes!).

A little under two hours later, the coffee and Eris have done their job. I blink awake as Eris—who I just noticed is wearing a sundress in the exact baby pink of zis elbow-pit vulva-rose tattoo (honestly, a flattering color for zis tan skin)—pulls into a rest stop. I am awake, I need to piss, and we're almost to Wisconsin, so it's my turn to drive the rest of the way. It's not entirely even, but there are no tolls or confusing interchanges to navigate from here. It's a fair swap.

The problem with being awake and paying attention is that I can't tune out Eris's constant chatter, most of it at my expense. Ze talks *so* much, reading every sign out loud, guessing what the roadkill used to be in graphic detail, and calling all the hawks perched along the freeway "falcons," even though they've all *clearly* been red-tails.

It's when ze points to a bird in the distance and declares it to be a bald eagle that I lose my patience at how confidently incorrect ze is. "Oh my god, it's a turkey vulture! *Not* an eagle!"

"Oh, you *can* speak!" Eris squints through the windshield. "How do you know it's a vulture?"

I fish my binoculars from the side pocket—proving exactly why I have them there—and pass them to zim.

Eris holds the binoculars up without removing the lens caps. "I can't see anything."

I snatch them back. "There's another pair in the glove box." The pair in the glove box are the ones I used as a kid. But if ze can't even figure out the lens caps on my nice pair, then ze can use the little kid binoculars. I wait for Eris to find the turkey vulture again before I explain, "You see how the wings are tippy as it coasts? That's a sign of a turkey vulture. Also, there are two of them, and they tend to be in pairs because they're monogamous for life.

Also, they're actually bald, unlike the bald eagle, which has a white head, unless it's a juvenile."

"Dude, you're a certified nerd. You're full of nature shit *and* law shit."

Eris's tone almost sounds respectful, and I'm tempted to see what expression goes with it. But I keep my eyes on the vultures. And the road, of course. "Pretty intentional considering I plan on working in environmental law, yeah."

"Why?"

Confused, I frown. "Why what?"

"Why are you going into environmental law?" Eris puts the binoculars back and snaps the glove box closed. "As your fake hot piece of ass, this is something I should know."

I frown harder, because ze's right. I hate talking about myself; it gives people ammunition. With this six-hour drive of uninterrupted time to talk looming all week, I've been putting off sharing anything Eris might need to know. But we're two hours in, and I still haven't said a thing about myself.

I sigh. "Spite, mostly."

Eris laughs. "Valid. Keep talking."

I grumble quietly before answering, "Matt's parents don't really value higher education, but my mom is a professor. The importance of college is a point of contention in their long-standing feud as next-door neighbors. His parents made him start working for the family construction business right out of high school, even though he's a math wiz and wanted to be an astrophysicist." Hands clenching around the steering wheel, I swallow the resentment I have for the Jacobsons; Matt chose to fall in line, and he's happy with that choice. "Matt's someone who finds contentment in the cards he's been dealt. The grass is greener where you water it, in his opinion. I just think he'd be happier with flowers."

"Oh man, so the people-pleasing thing isn't just you?" Eris teases.

I snort. "Back home, I'm the black sheep."

"Jesus Christ," Eris grumbles, rubbing zis forehead.

"Anyway, his mom took every opportunity to diminish my choice to go to college—my environmental studies major, the extracurriculars I was in, everything. One semester, I did an independent study on the limitations of the Water Pollution Control Act, and I mentioned offhand how I'd like to do something related to environmental policy. His mom basically thought I was wasting my time. That I'd never get into grad school, find a job, or make any difference in the world. So I have to prove her wrong."

Taking a breath to calm my lingering bitterness, I tap the steering wheel. But Eris doesn't ask a follow-up question, so I keep talking. "Also, I'm good at it? I think anyway. Like, yeah, reading cases is boring, but I enjoy figuring out the meaning in the legalese and thinking through the practical application and impacts. Like, analyzing and predicting the gaps between the spirit of the law and the letter of the law to make better policy is fascinating. I'm kinda burnt out on school, but I think I'll enjoy the work once I'm done cramming."

"Adrienne said you're super smart." The hesitant tone in zis voice makes me glance over, but Eris merely looks out the window, which leaves me no choice but to conclude that Eris Garcia just *complimented* me.

"She did?" I perk up, trying and failing not to preen at the secondhand praise. "I get decent grades, but I'm not the best in the class, by any means."

"Yeah. I mean, she says you're quiet, but you pick up on shit quick," Eris mutters, then snorts. "Kinda weird, considering you don't pay attention to anything normally."

"Thanks," I deadpan, a little relieved that we're back to normal. "I wasn't aware y'all talked about me."

"'Y'all' sounds awful in your accent," Eris groans. "We woulda talked *with* you, but you never come to shit besides brunch."

I focus on the semi I'm passing to avoid answering. Adrienne invites me to her and Dream's house sometimes, or to their family get-togethers on holidays. But brunch is the only thing I feel like I can go to.

"Don't go quiet on me again, Bambi," Eris says, zis gravelly voice soft.

"You didn't ask a question."

"'You didn't ask a question,'" Eris mimics me, zis mocking tone nasal and pinched. "The implied question was why don't you ever hang out with us besides brunch? Like, if it's because you don't like me, I get it, but don't hold yourself apart because of me."

My chest seizes as I sputter; the people pleaser in me wants to deny everything and apologize, but I'm clueless as to what I'd be apologizing for. "What?"

Eris hesitates before murmuring, "Everyone likes you, but you keep us at arm's length. Dream thinks it's my fault, but Adrienne says you're just introverted. But if that's true, then why only go out in public instead of hanging out at their house, you know? I guess..." Zis sigh is heavy. "I just want to make sure it's not something I'm doing wrong."

Blinking, I struggle to process what Eris just said, replaying zis words over and over again. My guard down, the people pleaser wins. "Sorry. I didn't mean to make everyone feel bad."

"Oh my god," Eris groans. "You always apologize for the most unnecessary shit, dude!"

"Sorry." I grin as ze smacks my arm. "I just... I can't have people over. Like, my place is too small, and frankly, messy, to have company."

Eris rubs zis forehead again. "What does that have to do with it?"

I blink in confusion. "Well, if they invite *me* over for dinner, I need to invite them back. And I didn't realize that *you all*," I emphasize my long vowels and the space between the words, making Eris snort, "hung out together like that, and I can't host that many people—"

"Wait," Eris interrupts. "So you don't come to their house because you can't reciprocate?"

"Well, and I didn't think anyone cared if I came or not," I mumble, my chest aching.

I can feel Eris's stare of confusion as I drive. "Bro, and I thought *I* was stupid."

Screwing my face up to hide the burning in my eyes, I spit out an offended, "Excuse you?"

"You think I invite anyone over? Or *Stella* does? Hell no! Dream likes to host shit, so we end up at her and Adrienne's house." Eris pokes the side of my head. "We all want to be your friend, you just have to let us. Show up sometimes. Open up, and talk about yourself more."

Fighting another apology, I swat zis hand away from my face. "I talk about myself!"

Eris catches my fingers. "Barely. When Dream makes you, you share facts about your life, but you don't tell us anything real."

"Oh, like *you're* any better?" Why is Eris still holding my hand? Why am I letting zim? Why can't I pull away from the strangely comforting grip?

"Look, I'm emotionally repulsive as a defense mechanism, but I joke about my trauma enough that my friends don't feel shut out. I open up more about heart-to-heart shit in private, not at brunch." Eris scoffs, pulling my hand towards zim. "You're just a pushover who can't set boundaries, so you tell people the barest facts when they ask, instead of telling them you don't wanna talk about it. Getting you to share your feelings or opinions about anything is like pulling teeth."

Zis hand still holds mine, thumb warm against my knuckles and zis grip grounding me. Unwilling to pull away, I keep my eyes firmly on the road. Quietly, I admit, "I don't know how to make friends. And, well..." I hesitate, but if this is how Eris makes friends, then I can share my real feelings. Ze sees the real me already, and ze still volunteered to accompany me to this impending catastrophe. "No one will like me if I open up. I'm not all that nice."

My jaw clenches; it sounds so pathetic.

My thoughts must be broadcasting directly to Eris, because ze says, "Do you hear how pathetic that sounds?"

I groan, fighting the urge to bash my forehead into the steering wheel. "Yeah, and I'm not proud of it."

"No one cares if you're *nice*." Derision drips from Eris's voice at the very idea. "Kelsey is a gossipy ass bitch, Stella is a complete brat, Adrienne can be manipulative as hell, and

Dream is so damn pushy! None of them are 'nice' either, why do you think you have to be?"

"Don't forget yourself! You're an asshole," I add, hoping to redirect the conversation to a subject where Eris isn't examining my heart under a microscope.

Eris chuckles half-heartedly. "Look, Bambi, I'm warning you now that I'm about to drag your ass everywhere. This whole time, everyone thought you were just shy and shit, or they told me I hurt your feelings because you're sensitive. But no, you're just fucking clueless."

I tsk, fighting a smile, my chest tight and warm in a way that can't be explained away by my binder. Chicago is nothing like Solberg. I thought Adrienne was just being nice because I didn't have any friends. But maybe I could have friends; I just have to trust that they'll still like me if I drop my facade.

Starting with Eris, who is still holding my hand, which is weird, but nice. I should get used to it. Over the next two days, I'm going to have to hold zis hand a lot. That ze wants to be my friend, wants to be my fake date for this wedding, still seems irrational; Eris has seen through my forced politeness from the start.

"You know, it's a miracle you came out, considering what a weak ass bitch you are," Eris scoffs. "Seriously, you don't let yourself take up any space unless someone invites you in like a damn vampire, and yet you're out of the closet?"

I shrug, because I see zis point. "I told you, in my town, I'm the rebel."

"Nah." Eris shakes zis head. "There's no way they're worse than you."

I shrug again, and to my shame, my shoulders get caught around my ears. "Small town mentality."

"I grew up in a small town too, and no way was it *that* bad."

I bite back my skepticism. Eris seems so at home in the city, our definition of a small town must be different. "Your town must not have been ninety percent Norwegian Lutherans," I retort instead, softened by zis thumb rubbing across my knuckles.

Out of the corner of my eye, Eris turns toward me, adding zis other hand to clasp mine completely between zis. The knuckles reading "amor" and "odio" interlace between my fingers. Ze inhales, as if ze's about to say something else. But I spot my first landmark in the distance.

"Look." Eager to change the subject, I point with the hand ze holds, half-hoping ze lets go. Eris doesn't, and the other half of me doesn't mind. "See that ridge?"

Eris hums in assent, looking out the window at the small hills stretching into the distance.

"That's a glacial moraine. That's where the glaciers left all the dirt and rocks that got ground up during the ice age."

Eris lets me change the subject. "So the part we just left wasn't under the glaciers?"

"It was, just a different ice age. We started in the Lake Michigan lobe, and now we're in the Green Bay lobe."

"Such a nerd, Bambi," Eris says, so softly it sounds like a compliment.

My response is cut short by an incoming phone call. Eris connected zis phone to my car before we left; ze figured my taste in music was boring. I let zim because it is.

"You speak Spanish?" Eris asks.

I shake my head. I took Latin as my foreign language, which is entirely useless for conversing, but helpful for both environmental studies and legal doctrine. "Allie minored in Spanish, so I can kind of read it, but I can't follow a conversation at all."

"Cool. Don't talk. It'll confuse her." Finally letting go of my hand, Eris presses the accept button. "Bueno, Abuelita."

"Erik, cielo mio!"

"Erisss, Abuelita," ze corrects her gently, and that is the extent of the conversation I can follow because Eris talks very fast. But ze sounds almost sweet talking to her. I've never heard zis voice so gentle. They laugh together, and their laughs are so similar that I can't help but smile as we pass Madison. Thankfully, the midmorning traffic on the freeway is light. The city used to feel huge compared to Solberg, but after two years in Chicago, it looks quaint and diminutive.

Is this the Eris I've been missing out on? Or would ze still be abrasive, even in the privacy of Adrienne's home? Or zis apartment, if we ever get to be close enough?

As I scold myself for letting *that* thought formulate, the peaceful conversation is interrupted by another woman, her voice sharp and cold as she cuts in. "Erik, I told you to stop bothering your grandmother."

In the background, zis grandma sounds agitated.

Eris huffs. "I'm not bothering her. We were having a good conversation until you—"

But the call ends before Eris can finish zis sentence.

Seven

LOVE DARTS

THE MUSIC RETURNS, BUT the silence is heavy between us. Keeping my eyes on the road, I wait, giving Eris room to open up if ze chooses. Strangely, I kind of want zim to make good on the heart-to-heart ze referenced before. But the silence stretches on.

"There's a drumlin over there," I say tentatively. "It's a glacial hill."

"You don't have to change the subject." Zis voice is thick. "You can ask questions if you're curious."

"You don't have to explain. Or you can? If you want?"

Eris laughs. "Yeah, that's how conversations work, Bambi."

I huff. "Just... Don't feel like you have to talk about anything unless you want to."

"Chill out. I'm just giving you shit." Ze slumps back in the passenger seat, bunching the hem of zis sundress in a clenched fist. "My grandma has dementia. Early on, she made reminders for herself to call her family. I always answer when she does, because it means she's lucid and lonely enough to miss the people she loves, even if she doesn't remember exactly who she's calling. But she gets confused easily, and she gets upset when she's confused."

That explains the uncharacteristically gentle tone in Eris's voice. "So you have to come out to her every time she calls, or be deadnamed the whole conversation?"

Eris nods. "I've got the delivery down pretty good by now."

"I'm sorry." I put my hand on Eris's this time.

Zis fist relaxes, letting go of the cotton skirt to lace our fingers together instead. "Stop apologizing. I'm used to it."

"Who hung up on you?"

"My mom."

Surprised, I glance at Eris, whose jaw clenches.

"I'm not welcome back home until I 'get my act together.' So be less embarrassing, basically. Not so visibly queer. A respectable cis man, discreet about who I sleep with, if I must 'choose' to be bisexual." Ze scoffs. "So no one ever contacts me, except Abuelita. It's nice that someone in my family reaches out, even if she doesn't actually remember who I am."

I never know how to sound sympathetic, but I can't not say *something* to that. "That sounds tough, Bud."

After our murmured conversation, Eris's cackle is like a tree trunk splitting in the dead of winter. The high-pitched laugh is less irritating after hearing zis grandma has the same one. "Jesus Christ! Good thing you're not a therapist, Bambi."

"I don't know what to say, and you told me to stop saying sorry!" I snap, pulling my hand away. "Thoughts and prayers! Is that better?"

With a grin, Eris grabs my hand and laces zis fingers through mine again. "I'm just giving you shit, dude. Awkward sympathy accepted and appreciated."

After a moment's silence, I say, "You don't talk about yourself often."

"You never ask me anything."

"I figure you'll share whatever you want to tell me."

Eris hums, and I'm not sure if that tone means ze agrees or not. "Hang out with us besides brunch, then. Hard to talk about real shit when we get interrupted by drag queens every few minutes."

I hum back, equally unsure if *I'm* agreeing or not. "So, what should I know about you? Since we've been dating for a few months and all."

"Right," Eris chuckles sardonically. "What do you want to know?"

Besides dragging up the apparently touchy subject of why Eris chose zis pronouns, I'm mostly curious about why Eris stopped tattooing. But ze didn't answer the last time I asked about it directly. "Work history? Education?"

"Is this a job interview?" Eris laughs again, and I can't help but smile along. "My dad comes from this old rancher family, and my mom basically transformed his inheritance into this farming empire. I went to school for agriculture because she expected me to expand the family business, but college was...freeing. Being queer wasn't in Mom's plans for me. Hard to break ground with conservative farmers in Texas when your successor is trans, you know? So after I finished my master's, I moved here and got a tattoo apprenticeship, instead of working for my parents because I wouldn't go back in the closet. Haven't really talked to my family since." Zis hand tightens around mine. "I dunno. Same sob story lots of queer people have, but I'm lucky. I grew up well-off, no college debt, got a degree in something useful."

I frown, heart lurching at how much pain Eris must have been through to speak about it so nonchalantly. "But family is important. They should still be there for you." I want to say something more sympathetic, but Eris will probably just tease me again, so I give up. "That's fucked up that they're not."

Eris snickers. "You had a really good childhood, didn't you, Bambi?"

I huff. "Why do you say that like it's an insult?"

"Just jealous. Can't relate to all that secure attachment."

Instead of downplaying it like a more polite person probably would (because my childhood was pretty great, sorry not sorry), I nod to the rolling hills and the forest on our left. "You see that?"

"Are those glacial trees?" Eris snarks.

"No, the opposite, actually!" I snort. "This is my favorite ecological region, the Driftless Area. This region was never covered during the last ice age, so it escaped the glaciation process. Basically, it's really pretty and hilly and very fun to drive through." I turn my blinker on and take the branch of the freeway leading toward the hills that will bring me back home. "Maybe on the way back, we can take the backroads so you can really appreciate it."

"If you want to spend more time with me by then, Bambi, I'm along for the ride."

We drive in silence a while longer, until I remember I'm supposed to be asking questions. But I only have one question— Well, two. But I am still minding my own damn business with the pronouns. "So why did you quit tattooing?"

Eris flexes the hand that isn't holding mine. "Arthritis. Easier to manage the pain when I'm not hunched over and clenching a vibrating needle machine for six hours a day."

That was not the reason I was expecting. "Uh... Wait, how old are you?"

Ze laughs. "That is definitely something you should know after a few months of dating! I'm only thirty-two, just overworked myself. How old are you?"

"Twenty-five," I admit, wondering if Eris will think I'm immature instead of an asshole.

"Damn, and you're already done with law school?" Eris once again sounds impressed with me, and I don't know how to handle it.

I shrug. "I moved here a week after I finished under-grad."

"That's dedicated. Working is gonna be a culture shock for you." Eris adds, "Do you have any tattoos? Or pierc-ings?"

I stiffen. "No piercings."

Oh, I can practically *hear* zim smile. "Oh? But you have tattoos?" When I don't speak, or even look at zim (be-cause I'm trying not to squirm, burning with preemptive embarrassment), Eris adds in a smug tone, "I'm assuming your Matt would know about this, and he might be con-fused why I don't."

With a sigh, I admit, "I have a tramp stamp."

Eris squeals, a new sound for me. "I'm so proud! What of?"

Another sigh as I keep my eyes forward. "A snail."

"Bambi, what the fuck?" Eris's laugh is delighted. "A snail? That's amazing!"

"They're really interesting, okay?" My huff is defensive. "They are biologically—as in Capital B Biology the science—bisexual, so they're both male and female. Also, they're cute, and they have eyestalks, and a spiral shell, and penises *and* vaginas, and they stab each other during foreplay, and I think they're just really neat."

Eris laughs the whole time I ramble, eventually pulling up the hem of zis dress with our joined hands to show me (a frankly hideous) cartoon snail on zis thigh. Zis leg hair is coarse on the back of my knuckles as I graze Eris's bare skin, and I'm curious what it'd feel like under my fingertips. "I did this one as practice for my linework when I had no idea what the fuck I was doing."

That spiral does *not* follow the Fibonacci ratio, and the eyes are *between* the upper and lower tentacles. I frown, because that is my pet peeve; the whole point of the upper tentacles is the eyestalks. "That's...cute." I turn back to the road so ze can't see my judgmental expression (and to remove any temptation to touch it). My snail looks *way* better than that.

"Matt ever come on yours?"

"Excuse me?!" I cough.

"You know, the slime. 'Cause it's a snail. He ever pull out during backshots and just paint the shit out of it? Turn that thing into a toaster strudel?"

My whole body burns. "No!"

"Shame. That's the fun of a tramp stamp! Waste of a weird tattoo." I refuse to look away from the road, but I know Eris is wearing that shit-eating smirk. "So, Bambi, tell me about your relationship with Matt. How you got together, why you broke up, your unhealthy codependent friendship now, the freaky shit y'all used to do together. All of it."

I wrinkle my nose. "Do I have to?"

"Of course not," Eris murmurs, then adds, "Look, from what you've said, he's a tall Adonis with a heart of gold. He's going to wonder why you think I'm an upgrade, so give me something to keep up my sleeve when he tries to intimidate me."

"He wouldn't do that," I scoff.

"He wouldn't do that to *you*!" Eris snarks back, then softens. "I'm not weaponizing your relationship, just wanna know what I'm walking into."

I huff because I want Eris to be wrong, but ze isn't. "Fine. We grew up next door to each other, high school sweethearts, stayed together in college. Broke up because he didn't want to do long distance. He was and always will be my best friend, and he fell in love with my other best friend after I left, so now they are still my best friends. Just...more of a unit."

"Those are *facts*, Bambi. This is the shit I was talking about." Eris tsks. "Open up a little. Give me your *feelings*, your hopes and dreams, your fears and regrets."

"Gross," I grumble, glaring at the road. "Matt had quieter dreams than I did."

"Good, that's a nice start. Elaborate." Eris waves our joined hands expectantly.

"Like I said, he's someone who doesn't see the grass on the other side as greener because he's always excited to water his own grass." I hesitate, but push myself to keep talking, to get to the feelings Eris won't stop asking for. "The issue was that *I* wanted flowers, for both of us, and Allie. And not just a little garden, I wanted fields of wildflowers. For me, and him, and her, and for us, and I pushed him to dream more." I sigh. "Turns out, he was never a dreamer, but he respected my dreams more than I did. When I got cold feet about leaving, he broke up with me so he wouldn't hold me back. Told me to spread my gay little wings and move to Chicago and go save the world." I clench my jaw. I hate talking about this, because how *dare* Matt make that decision for me?

And why could I not make that decision for myself?

After the accident, I was filled with determination to live life to the fullest, to not miss a moment, to make all my dreams come true. But other than Matt, no one else wanted me to live it. Everyone in Solberg, including my parents, insisted on keeping me safe, fencing in all my ambition under the guise of protection. I let them mow me down. Applying to law school was a seed burst from a moment of anger, fortunate to sprout in my simmering resentment. Only Matt watered it, even when I was ready to let it wither.

"Did you know he was in love with Allie?" Eris asks.

I shook my head. "I don't think he was, not yet. She was in love with him, though she never admitted it. When he broke up with me, I left right away because a clean break would let them figure their shit out sooner. They deserve each other, and Allie only had a three-month internship before she ran out of excuses to stay, and this was her chance for a happier life than she would have if she moved back in with her family."

Eris sits silently before quietly asking, "Did they know you're in love with her, too?"

"I'm not." I shake my head, unwilling to ask how ze figured out a secret I never shared with anyone, one I've barely admitted to myself. Even in the throes of my guilt and confusion about the girl who stole my heart freshman year, when it was supposed to belong to Matt and Matt alone. "Not anymore, anyway. I love them both, but I'm no longer in love with either of them. When Matt and I were still together, I hinted at it sometimes. But Matt is built for monogamy, and Allie is too straight to consider me a possibility."

Eris hums sympathetically. "This is the most tragic love triangle. You want a triad, but they form a line without you."

I laugh, and it sounds wetter than I want. But Eris's thumb swipes over my knuckles again, and the ache in my chest eases. "Exactly. But I've had two years to process it, and trips home during breaks, so we've hung out enough to get comfortable again. I am genuinely happy for them, and they still love me, just in a new way."

Eris's hum sounds strangely like my mother's when she's about to change the subject. "So, how was the sex, then? Missionary, no talking? Did he give trash head? Try to stick it in the back without prep and pretend it was an accident?"

"What the fuck, Eris?" I laugh, relieved to lighten the mood. "It was fine!"

"Fine?"

"Fine!" I know Eris is waiting for more, because *fine* is never fine. "Just a little tame. Mostly missionary, more kissing than talking, and only the nice things that nice guys say during sex. Head was good, but he was not remotely interested in anal, for him or me."

"Oh, Bambi. You poor thing," Eris teases.

"I know. I shouldn't complain. Like, he was really generous and...nice."

"No, no, I wasn't being sarcastic!" Eris tsks. "You *can* complain about that! Sounds vanilla as hell. Did you ever tell him you wanted more?"

"Yeah, I asked him to try dirty talk." I fight a smile at the memory. "He got as far as calling me a good girl when I blew him, but that ended when I came out a non-binary. We couldn't find a good alternative."

Ze chuckles knowingly. "What did he call you?"

I sigh. "He called me a good person."

Eris's shrieking cackle makes me laugh, even though it shouldn't because Matt tried *so* hard. He just never understood what I was asking for. It's a little funny in hindsight, but it was painfully awkward then.

When we can breathe again, Eris pulls my hand to zis face, resting zis cheek against it. The stubble scrapes my palm, and I flex my hand to cup zis jaw more firmly. "So what, you wanted him to call you a little slut and spank you?"

"Not necessarily, but that would have been cool." I squirm, skin hot. But if Eris and I are going to fake happiness, this stuff might be useful. "Just... I didn't need for him to whisper that he loved me in my ear every time he came. Like, it was sweet, and sometimes the mood was right for that. But again, we're back to how I wanted more, and he couldn't give that to me. So he let me go."

Eris's lips press to my wrist, sucking on my pulse oh so lightly. The flutter against my skin makes it hard to breathe, my binder growing constricting instead of comforting. "So he never told you to get on your knees and choke on his cock?"

That deep gravelly voice, saying those words...

My muscles clench from my thighs to my shoulders, and the car veers onto the shoulder. The rumble strips are loud beneath the tires until I jerk us back to center. "I'm trying to drive!" Burning hot, I try to yank my hand away.

Eris holds on tight. "But, Bambi, you blush so pretty."

I wince, quickly masking it, but Eris sees. Of course, Eris sees.

"Not pretty?"

I shake my head, eyes trained on the car ahead of me, not sure I want to see the expression on Eris's face. To see if ze's truly flirting, or simply mocking me. "Not cute, either."

"Not pretty, not cute. Cool." Eris finally lets go of my hand. Reluctantly, I bring it back to the steering wheel. My palm and fingers are cold. Strange, when the rest of my body is still blazing. "That gives me enough to work with."

"Work with?" Why do I sound out of breath?

"Enough to whisper in your ear when people are looking, enough to put any doubts to rest that we're not really together."

Oh. Right. My chest tightens with embarrassment, and I don't want to think about what the empty drop of my stomach really means.

"It's a shame, though," Eris says. "When a relationship that should work doesn't because of incompatibility. Same thing happened with me and Stella."

Like ice water, I'm doused with the reminder that I barely know Eris. "You dated Stella?"

Eris hums. "A few years ago. We didn't last long. I'm not as vanilla as your Matt, but by queer standards, I'm barely kinky. And Stella is pretty hardcore, like extreme masochism, degradation, pup play, that sort of thing. We tried, but we couldn't find common ground, so we decided to stay friends instead. They just moved in with their handler though, so everything worked out well for them." Ze shrugs.

"Stella?" I sputter. They're so timid, but I have no reason to doubt Eris, so I just add that to the very short list of facts I know about Stella. "Is that why you're so mean to them?"

Eris's gasp is offended. "I am *not* mean to them! They're such a brat all the time!"

"How? Last time we went to brunch, they said something poetic and wise, and you threw your napkin at them."

"That was *not* poetic and wise—what the fuck? They were..." Eris growls in annoyance. "You know what? Never mind. Sure. Stella is poetic and wise, and I'm a raging dick! Let's go with that!"

"If you have a diff—"

"Nope. Let's change the subject."

"Fine." I replay our conversation, wondering what to ask. "Give me something, too?"

"Give you something, what?"

I mull over my words, wondering how to even the playing field without sounding desperate, even though I want to turn Eris into a squirming mess too. "What do I need to whisper in your ear, so people believe us?"

"Oh my god, I hate you." Eris lets out a strangled sigh. "Do *not* tell anyone this, but I kind of have a praise kink."

"You?" I laugh, but stop when Eris doesn't join me. "Sorry. That's not funny?"

"No, I get it," Ze scoffs. "Like I said, I'm emotionally repulsive as a defense mechanism. So when people aren't repelled... It's nice." Eris's hands go back to twisting zis hemline, and I fight the urge to reach out, to take them in mine again instead.

"So, you want me to say you look pretty in that dress?" I ask, somewhat hesitantly. "Or that I like your laugh?"

Eris is quiet for a moment. "Only if you mean it. Like, don't lie."

"I do," I glance over to see Eris staring hard at zis lap, delighting at how much ze is fidgeting from a mere hesitant compliment, as ze crosses and recrosses zis legs at the ankle. "Thank you for coming with me, Eris. I'm glad you're here, that we're doing this together."

"Oh my god, stop." The light brown skin behind the scattered stars along zis cheekbones flushes, zis lips pressed between zis teeth.

Determined to see how flustered I can make zim this weekend, I start silently listing ways I might praise Eris, a smug smile on my face. Surprisingly, considering how much energy I've dedicated to analyzing everything I don't like about zim, the things I appreciate about Eris flow like a spring, and I add compliment after compliment to my mental list.

Eight

MATT

WHEN WE ARRIVE AT the hotel in "Downtown" Solberg, I park under an old basswood to protect my car from the hot June sun. The air is sweet from the fields and woods around town, with a cold undercurrent from the river that winds past the hotel. Leaning against the door, I stretch out my stiff leg. My heart swells as I bask in the familiar comfort of the brick buildings and cute shops lining Main Street.

Being here feels too easy, too normal. Especially with Eris in tow, who doesn't fit into my mental image of home. We get a few looks from people driving by, which is to be expected anytime there's a stranger in Solberg. At this point, I may as well be one myself, and Eris sticks out like a sore thumb. Zis baby pink sundress (paired with combat boots) leaves the weird tattoos and hairy chest on full display as we grab our bags from the car.

And yet, I feel no dissonance.

It's so peaceful and right and everything I missed. The townies passing by probably assume we're with the college when they ignore us. Things between Eris and I have gotten almost comfortable after six hours sharing everything about ourselves. So comfortable that I forget that I'm supposed to be dreading this.

As strong, familiar arms wrap around my waist and whirl me in circles without warning, I remember that this weekend won't be as easy as the car ride here.

When Matt sets me down amidst our laughter, Eris's face is tense, unreadable. Ze stares up at Matt, who is all goofy excitement and unabashed joy in contrast. Is Eris acting the part of a jealous partner? Or is ze actually upset? Maybe ze's anxious?

"What the hell is this, Bloke?" With a scoff, Matt snatches a pair of black heels out of my hand. I was in the middle of stuffing them back into Eris's tote bag when he picked me up. "You're not wearing these are you?"

"So what if they are?" Eris asks, voice sharp.

Glancing at me in panic, Matt stiffens, his boyish enthusiasm draining away. "Because you're gonna be limping for weeks!" He elbows me with a more forced attempt at cheer. "Remember prom, dude? I had to carry you home, and those were flats!"

"What Blake wears or doesn't wear is none of your business." Eris's scarred eyebrow raises at me, and my insides squirm. Maybe I should have told Eris about my knee.

"Kinda is, though." Matt shifts back and forth, the way he does when his conflict-avoidant ass wants to run away from a tense conversation. "I'm not letting them reinjure their knee at the wedding I invited them to."

With a confused frown, Eris cocks zis head. "That's a weird way to phrase it. It's *your* wedding, isn't it?"

I still can't tell if Eris is acting the part or just being a dick, but I'm over it. Eris is here to be an abrasive weirdo, yes, but not to *Matt*. Ze and I might be friends now, and if we are, I want my friends to get along. "Eris, you said you weren't gonna be an asshole."

Ze snorts. "No, *you* said that. My assholery is part of my charm."

I scowl, uncaring if Matt thinks it's weird that we're not all lovey-dovey. If he calls me out, I'll come up with something about how not every relationship is the same. "Well, I don't need you to speak for me. Let *me* tell Matt off for telling me what to wear."

Eris gives me a long look, then smirks and ruffles my hair. "Look at you, advocating for yourself. Proud of you, Bambi!"

"Shut up!" I smack zis hand away.

Matt looks back and forth between us, the gap between his teeth visible as he relaxes into his usual charming grin. "Oh my god, ze is perfect for you!"

"Can you not?" I smack him, too. "Anyway, no introduction needed I guess, but Matt, Eris. Eris, Matt."

"Great to meet you, dude!" Matt waves the heels in greeting, before his smile tightens into a wince. "Wait, can I call you dude? Sorry. I call everyone dude, but I can call you something else if it bothers you. Just let me know, and I'll get it right. Sorry."

"Oh god, he *is* worse than you," Eris mutters under zis breath. "Call me whatever. I don't care. Just chill out." Ze snatches zis heels back from Matt, who nods furiously, overeager as always. "And for the record, these are mine.

Not everyone is a corn-fed himbo like you two. I like having a few extra inches."

"Don't we all," I mutter before Eris's meaning sinks in. "Wait, I'm not a himbo!"

Eris merely smirks at me.

Hips rocking side to side now (a sign that he's "chilled out"), Matt beams. "Love that! You have great style, by the way. Just really yourself! I think that's amazing and courageous to march to the beat of your own drum like you do. Your dress is really cute! I like your tattoos too! So edgy! How many do you have? What's your favorite one? Which one hurt the most?"

To my utter delight, Eris's cheeks flush again. Zis mouth hangs open as Matt rambles, blurting out questions and compliments like confetti.

"Matt, take a breath," I tease. "Can we check in before you interrogate zim?"

Matt reddens. "Sorry. Got carried away." He fishes in his pocket and passes me a room key. "Here. Sorry, you're right next door to my parents. So, good luck!" He makes finger guns at us with a click of his tongue.

"Oh god," I groan.

"Amazing!" Eris snatches the room key from me. "Bambi, I'm gonna pull a noise complaint or two out of you this weekend."

"Eris!" It's my turn to blush furiously as Matt and Eris both crack up. "What the fuck? Why are you like this?"

"On that note, my parents still don't know you're coming." Matt tries and fails to hide his glee. Even if he bends to his parents will, he still finds ways to push back against them. Just in little ones that he could play off as ignorance. "So, like, have fun? No need to hold anything back, if you know what I mean." He winks with another click of his tongue. "Anyway, I'm probably running late to the rehearsal, so I'll see you two at the groom's dinner thing later! If you beat us there, please record my mom's reaction!"

As soon as Matt is out of earshot, Eris leans toward me. "Gotta be honest, I was hardcore judging you for being so hung up on your ex—"

"I'm not hung up on him."

Eris ignores me, hefting zis bag over zis shoulder. "But I get it now. I would probably never let that man go either. He's so...nice. I hate that word, but that's what he is."

I shut the hatchback of my station wagon with a sigh. "Don't forget, you're the upgrade."

We both wave as Matt drives past us out of the parking lot, heading to Sigurdsson's campus where the wedding will be tomorrow afternoon. He bumps the curb, too busy cheesing at us and waving wildly to pay attention to where he's going.

"Yeah, but I'm not *that*," Eris mutters. "He's so hot and awkward, I just feel compelled to protect him and keep him safe from the world."

"I dunno, you're pretty great, Bud," I tease, putting my hand on the small of zis back as we head toward the front of the hotel. A hint of fluster tinges Eris's tattooed cheeks, and I can't help but smile. "You have great style."

"Shut the fuck up."

"So courageous," I murmur in zis ear. "So cute and edgy."

"Bambi, I will shut you up if you keep this up." Eris glares at me, zis face flushed dark red. My cheeks burn at the warning in zis eyes, but my grin only widens. "I regret telling you anything."

Nine

Home Sweet Home

It should feel ugly, the cold satisfaction that curls in my belly when Mrs. Jacobson sees me walk into the rehearsal dinner. But I love every second. The double take, the flash of shock and anger before her perfect mask is back on. Unobtrusive for once, Eris trails behind me. My presence alone was enough to make her facade crack, just for a second; my chest glows in delight.

The Cheery Chicken (the bar where every large gathering in Solberg is held, because it's the only restaurant that rents out the back patio that overlooks the river for private events) is a few blocks from our hotel. Even that short walk was a reminder that I no longer belong here. Between the bemused looks from people who pretended not to recognize me, and the comments about the weather that strangers exchange in lieu of greetings, Eris quickly agreed with me that Solberg is a small town rendition of *The Stepford Wives*.

So the Jacobsons fit right in. Rushing through the crowded patio, Matt's mom greets me too loudly, too friendly to be genuine. "Blake! I had no idea you would be here!" She gives me an air kiss, her fingers gripping tight on my forearms.

"Last minute addition." I return her faux-enthusiasm in kind, my own hands forming claws around her wrists. After a lifetime of being her neighbor, my fake side comes naturally. My forced smile turns simpering, so Mrs. Jacobsen can't ignore that I'm putting on the same airs she is. "My invitation must have been lost in the mail. Happened to my parents, too!" I screw my face up in dramatized confusion. "Strange, I wonder how that could have happened?"

Her eyes flash, but her plastic smile stays put. "Yes, well. You showed up anyway!"

"I wouldn't miss this for the world!" Causing any hint of this woman's anger fills me with delight. The spiteful shell that protected me from Mrs. Jacobson's passive-aggressive suggestions and backhanded compliments my whole childhood is no longer mere armor. My resentment has grown petty roots in my heart, nearly as nourishing and motivating as my parents' love.

Mrs. Jacobson's eyes slide over to Eris, who comes around to stand next to me in zis full genderfuck glory. Her perfect smile slips in shock. To my surprise, my gut reaction isn't that cold satisfaction. In its place, a surge of protectiveness makes my stomach clench. How dare this bitch look at Eris with disdain?

Despite the curl of her lip, Eris stands proudly. A smirk teases the corners of zis mouth as ze and Mrs. Jacobson stare at each other.

Her sneer hits harder because Eris looks positively classy for once, with a sleeveless black turtleneck, neatly trimmed mustache, and a turquoise pendant and earrings that match zis septum ring. The tattoos on Eris's skull are sharp and vibrant thanks to a fresh undercut. Zis tight black jeans, tucked into heeled boots, emphasize the shapeliness of zis thick calves. Eris's makeup is immaculate, the flower in zis chignon charming.

I wrap my arm around zis waist, pulling zim close. "Oh, where are my manners! This is Eris. Eris, this is Matt's mother, Mrs. Jacobson." Twenty years as neighbors, and I'm still not allowed to call her by her first name.

"Pleasure to meet you, ma'am." Eris holds out a hand, which Mrs. Jacobson gingerly shakes. Her nostrils flare in a sharp sniff as she reads the "And I Say, Fuck It!" script tattooed on zis forearm. "Blake has told me so much about you."

"Good things, I hope," Mrs. Jacobson's fake laugh is as annoying as ever.

Eris merely shrugs, which I deeply appreciate.

Mrs. Jacobson's smile dims. "So, what do you do for work, Eris?"

"I'm a drug dealer."

I choke, sputtering out, "You are *not* a drug dealer!"

"I sell cannabis for recreational and medicinal use, Blake. Pretty sure I'm a drug dealer."

"Ze manages a licensed dispensary," I cough out, trying to reassure Mrs. Jacobson that Eris is not a criminal. Her very strong opinions on marijuana haven't changed since the Reagan administration. She is the reason my parents grow and smoke exclusively in the basement; she would absolutely call the DEA. Even though it's legal...now. I think. Actually, my parents are probably over the legal limit with how many plants they have.

Instead of engaging further in *that* conversation, Matt's mom looks to the entrance. "Oh, there's the happy couple! Finally!"

That's all the warning I have before Matt knocks into Eris and me again, like an overeager puppy. "Oh my god, you guys look so hot! You even dress alike!"

Eris and I exchange a confused look as Matt hugs us. I'm wearing a black linen button-up, adorned with a gold chain between the collar studs, and pleated shorts that hang past my knee. I guess we're both in black, and for Matt, that's apparently enough.

"Matt, I'm not sure you should call anyone but your bride-to-be 'hot' the night before you get married," Mrs. Jacobson hisses through a gritted smile. "Especially your ex!"

Matt smiles blankly, his usual answer when his mom says something he disagrees with.

A shriek of my name makes me turn just as another ball of energy collides with my middle, squeezing me tight. This ray of sunshine is all blond curls and vanilla perfume. White maxi dress swirling, Allie bounces in excitement. She steps back from crushing her face to my chest to give me a once-over. "Fuck, you look good! I missed your sexy ass!"

Before I can respond, she whirls to face Eris, enveloping zim in a hug before ze can react. "Oh my god, you must be Eris! I'm so jealous Matt got to meet you first!"

"Matt, Allie, darlings, your wedding isn't for socializing with your...friends." Mrs. Jacobson pries Allie away from Eris and nudges her towards Matt. "Go, mingle with your other guests! You'll have plenty of time to catch up with Blake and her friend. Later."

Allie's smile falls, and I want to punch Matt's mom.

"Their," Eris says, breaking the silence. "I'm *their*... Well, friend isn't the right word, but I'm *theirs*. Not *hers*."

My curl of satisfaction from the vein twitching in Mrs. Jacobson's temple twists into a glow of euphoria. Matt, despite correcting everyone else, has never corrected his parents. I've always been my own guard dog—and his—when it came to the Jacobsons. I have never expected anyone else to take up that mantle, especially not Eris.

I take Eris's hand and shoot zim an appreciative smile. "Weddings are to celebrate with loved ones, right? I'm sure people will understand if they spend some time with us."

"No, it's all right!" Allie insists, her smile twisting. She and Matt exchange a loaded glance when he puts a hand on her back. "We should go greet everyone, but I'll be back to hear all about you soon, Eris!"

Mrs. Jacobson herds them away. Matt and Allie send us twin exasperated looks over their shoulders, but follow her anyway.

"So that's Allie." I turn to Eris, who stares at me with a perplexed expression. Thanks to zis heels, ze's almost at eye level, and my self-consciousness blooms under zis close inspection. "What? Do I have something on my face?"

"Everything makes so much more sense now." Ze turns and heads to the bar.

"What does that mean?" I hurry after zim, careful not to let my gait dip; Matt would give me so much shit for barely doing my PT since I've moved. As we weave through the crowd, I recognize some of Matt's friends, but they pretend not to see me. Which I'm totally fine with. I'm more interested in debriefing with Eris than forcing a conversation with people who've barely spared me a thought in two years.

Eris ignores my question to order a glass of wine from the outdoor bar. The only other free option is beer, so I order the same. The place is crowded, as far as Solberg goes, and everyone has formed circles to socialize in. Joining them is always awkward, so Eris and I unspokenly weave around the cliques to find somewhere out of the way. When we've found a corner along the railing to occupy, I ask again. "What do you mean, it makes sense now?"

"Look, they're golden retrievers." Eris shrugs, taking in the sight of the small town clinging to the riverbank with interest. The waterfall upriver rushes over the dam. Ze jerks zis back toward Allie and Matt across the patio. "They're goofy, and cute, and eager to please, and want everyone to be happy, and they'll take it personally if you don't. No wonder you felt you had to prove you're not a sad fuck."

"I'm not a sad fuck," I lie. Because I am a sad fuck.

Eris gestures across the patio, where Matt and Allie have been roped into a conversation with his high school football coach. "These two ridiculously attractive sweethearts looked at you, with their puppy dog eyes, and begged for reassurance that they weren't ruining your life by getting together. And you pretend to be nice, so you had to make them stop feeling guilty for putting themselves first. It's all clear now!"

I smack zis arm. "I am nice!" I want people to think so, anyway.

Ze grins and smacks my arm right back. "In some ways, maybe. But you're no Matt and Allie. Which is good, because they must have the worst anxiety." Ze slurps zis wine. "And his mom is a piece of work. Gotta love control issues! Reminds me of my mom," Eris laughs. Zis loud, high-pitched cackle draws quite a few gazes.

I meet their looks with a set of my chin, daring them to say anything. Almost everyone looks away, because they're all small-town Lutherans. Avoiding conflict is a cultural norm here.

But one person looks back, her eyes narrowing.

If I hadn't already seen Allie, I would have done a double take. But this woman is wearing a blush pink version of Allie's white maxi dress, and the expression on her face is anything but the eager, bright-eyed grin that always made me feel like I belonged.

"Oh, god, incoming," I mutter, forcing a smile as Allie's bitchy twin sister makes a beeline for us. Eris slides zis hand into mine, lacing our fingers together. Zis reassuring strength helps me breathe a little easier as Jessica scurries between the clusters of people.

"What are you doing here?" she hisses in lieu of a hello.

"Jessica! How lovely to see you!" I repeat my fake-nice song and dance like I did for Matt's mom, my forced smile cold. "This is my... Eris! Eris, this is Allie's twin sister! And the maid of honor, right? How exciting, being the maid of honor for your twin!"

"You aren't supposed to be here." Jessica doesn't play along. She never does. Allie and Jessica are from Edina, but Allie fell in love with the quiet of Solberg. She dreaded moving home so much that my parents offered her the spare bedroom at our house, so she could stay longer. Not that she dislikes her sister—I doubt Allie could dislike anyone, and she loves her sister dearly—but college was the first time she could escape her family's smothering embrace.

"Allie and Matt invited me." I glower, dropping the nice act since Jessica isn't pretending either. Despite Allie's insistence otherwise, her sister has never liked me. From Jessica's perspective, I stole her twin. "Because *someone* stole my invitation."

Jessica crosses her arms, blue eyes cold. "You should have known better."

I shrug as Eris's hand squeezes mine in reassurance. "Their wedding, their guest list."

"Maybe *Matt* wants you here, but Allie doesn't," Jessica snips.

"Weird, it must have been a different Allie who mailed me a handwritten letter, begging me to come." I roll my eyes.

Jessica scoffs. "Allie doesn't know what she wants—"

"How old were you?" Eris interrupts.

"What?" Jessica glares at zim.

Eris smiles sweetly, cocking zis head. Voice bright and airy, ze asks, "How old were you when you realized you were the ugly twin?"

I snort as Jessica bristles. "We're identical," she says.

"On the outside, sure." Eris nods with a sympathetic pout.

Jessica huffs. "I don't know what game you think you're playing, but you need to leave."

"No, Matt and Allie want us here," I say, relieved when Allie notices us and rushes over to run interference.

"You won't get him back," Jessica snaps.

"What?" My heart drops; how could anyone possibly think I'm here to get Matt back?

"You're here to steal my sister's happiness, and I can't let you do that. This," she waves at Eris, "must be part of the plan to get him back."

"This is a person, thanks," Eris deadpans.

But I'm looking at Allie, who freezes a few feet away, staring right at me. Her blue eyes widen as her sister's words sink in.

Disbelief paralyzing me, I only manage to shake my head. Willing Allie to understand I would never want anything but the best for her and Matt, that I'm not there to cause trouble.

But Allie just looks back, her brow furrowed and her lips parted, trembling.

"Who would pick *you* over Matt? There's no way this is real."

Eris opens zis mouth to retort, but I break first. "Shut up, Jessica!" My eyes burn with hurt that Allie is listening to her sister's bullshit, from the anger at myself for lying in the first place. That ugly defensiveness for Eris rears its head, and my emotional turmoil gratefully takes a backseat. "Don't you dare talk to zim like that! Eris is incredible, and gorgeous, and funny. Just because you're jealous and bitter doesn't mean I am."

Jessica sputters. "I am not jealous!"

"You were jealous that Sigurdsson rejected you, jealous of any friend Allie's ever had, and now you can't stand that Allie's happier than you." The cold venom leaking into my voice is luscious. I might regret exposing my ugly side to Solberg's ridicule later, but right now I couldn't stop myself if I tried. "This wedding looks more like the one you'll never have than hers. Allie fucking hates pink, and if you cared about her more than yourself, you would get that by now." With a glare, I push past her, pulling Eris along behind me by the hand. "Let's go."

In my rush to escape, I stride right through the closed circles of conversation instead of going around, ignoring the mutters of how rude I am, comments on our appearance, questions of why Matt's ex is here. When I glance over my shoulder at all the judgmental eyes watching us leave, Allie is nowhere to be seen.

Ten

LAID BARE

"Dammit, Blake, wait." Eris's arm hooks around my waist, pulling me around the corner of the bar and into the alley. "Slow down. What the fuck."

With the brick wall against my back and Eris's hand on my chest to pin me there, I deflate. The anger and bitterness leaches out of me, embarrassment and humiliation taking its place. My eyes fill with hot tears, and my skin prickles with shame. "I'm sorry."

"No, don't do that, Bambi." Eris's hand slides from my chest to my waist, pulling me into a hug. "Don't apologize for them."

"I shouldn't have come. I shouldn't have brought you here." I wrap my arms around zis shoulders, burying my face in zis neck. Eris's chin finds a home in the crook of my shoulder, and ze strokes my back as I whisper, "I don't know why I thought this would be a good idea. It's humiliating. I just wanted to prove that I'm okay, that I'm happy for them, but everyone thinks I'm the attention-seeking ex who can't get over him. I'm so embarrassed."

"The only ones who should be embarrassed are Bitch One and Bitch Two."

Fighting a sob, I sniffle. "I don't belong here. I love this place, and my parents, and Matt and Allie, but I've never belonged here. Not with the rest of them."

"I know, Bambi." Eris sways us gently, zis voice calming and warm in my ear. "They're too small for you, but don't shrink yourself for them. You found two gems who look at you and see the angel you are, and the rest are terrified because your holiness is beyond their comprehension."

"Don't start being sweet now, Bud," I tease, laughing through my tears.

Eris's smile presses against my cheek. "You started it."

"I did not!"

"Incredible, you said." Eris pulls back, a twinkle in those doe eyes. The scars on zis lips go crooked as ze smirks. "Gorgeous, funny? Does that ring a bell?"

I huff. "Those are facts. Not cheesy metaphors."

Eris cups my cheek, a callous-rough thumb scraping my jawline. "Oh, facts? I see. Well, thank you for speaking the truth then. No one has ever stood up for me like that before."

My heart pounds in my throat. "Don't thank me! I'm the one who dragged you into this shitshow. You wouldn't have to put up with this bullshit if it weren't for me."

"Bambi, I knew what I was getting into," Eris murmurs. "And I did it anyway."

"But why?" I ask. "I've been awful to you. Not just now, but from the start."

"You really haven't been, but I like the inner sass you always hide," Eris teases, far more softly than I deserve. "I'm honored to witness you finally letting it out. You're too damn nice."

"I'm not nice," I insist, shaking my head. "You just saw what a petty bitch I can be."

"Okay. We can do this another way," Eris huffs. Zis exhale prickles the skin of my neck. "You're not nice, then. So what? Allie's cunt of a sister is a bitter jealous hag, and Matt's uptight controlling mom wants to erase you from his life. You're here to rock the boat *for* your friends, to reassure them that you're happy for them, not to split them up. And I'm here to help with that. Because even if it's not *polite*, that's a *kind* thing to do."

"No, I *wanted* to piss them off." Fresh tears well up again. "That's not kind at—"

"Bambi! Stop." Eris's grip on my jaw tightens, drawing my gaze to zis brown eyes, narrowed in annoyance. The inside of my cheek cuts into my teeth under the pressure of zis thumb. "Fine, you are selfish and spiteful and rude, but you love your friends. And those muppets frankly need someone like you to have their back. So don't get all bent out of fucking shape because things went the way you wanted." Eris steps closer, body pressing against mine. Zis husky voice resonates through my chest. "You need to tell yourself you're a petty bitch? Fine, you are. But you're petty for the right reasons, and more importantly, for this weekend, you're *my* bitch. And I won't let you spiral because small people can't handle you."

The pathetic, trembling whimper that leaves my lips is the most embarrassing thing that's happened yet on this trip—possibly in my entire life. But the thrill when Eris's eyes dip down to my mouth makes the humiliation worth it. My lips are pursed, pinched by the grip of zis fingers as Eris draws my face intoxicatingly close to zis.

"Oh Bambi," Eris breathes, a smile stretching slowly across zis face. "Did you like that?"

My grip on zis shoulders tightening, I scramble to pull Eris closer, to close the gap between us, to kiss zim like I think we both want to. But zis hold remains strong.

With a tsk, Eris crowds me against the brick wall, one knee fitting between mine. "Say it, Bambi. I used my words, you can use yours."

My breath grows shallow; too deep, and it would push Eris away when I need zim closer. I swallow hard. "Yes."

"Yes, what?"

"Yes, I liked it," I scoff. "Are you happy now?"

"Not quite yet," ze teases. "Did you like when I called you mine? Or when I called you a bitch?"

My thighs clench around Eris's. The quiet "both" that leaves my lips is raspy.

"So all this time, you just kept taking all my rude ass bullshit because you *liked* it?" At my reluctant nod, Eris grins, dark and full of promise. "And you kept that delightful information all to yourself?"

Unsure what to say, I wait, looking at Eris expectantly. Lovely as that smile is, that is not what zis mouth should be doing. Ze should be pressing me against this wall and stealing my soul through my lips. But Eris makes no move to end my impatient agony, keeping that tight grip on my jaw that I don't want to resist.

"There you are— Oh shit, I'm so sorry!"

God, Matt has the worst timing.

Eris presses a too-brief kiss to the corner of my lips, breathing quietly in my ear, "You were wasted on him," before pulling away to greet Matt. Considering I'm a trembling puddle slumped against the wall, it's unfair how casually ze waves Matt off. "No worries! We were just talking about heading back to the hotel early."

"Everything okay?" Matt asks, rubbing the back of his neck. For once, he's staying an awkward distance away, though the setting sun casts his shadow long enough to fall upon our feet. "Allie said... You left without saying goodbye."

The rush of irritating, confusing feelings floods through me again. Eris raises zis eyebrow at me, somehow sensing I'm back on the verge of spiraling. The scar, a stark interruption of zis thick brows, silently scolds me and reminds me I'm here for the right reasons, even if Allie doesn't understand them.

I put on a smile for Matt. "Yeah, sorry, my knee was acting up. Sorry."

"Your knee?" Matt instantly goes into mother-hen mode. It's annoying as always. "Do you want me to find some ibuprofen? Have you been doing your exercises?"

I huff. "Matt, I'm fine, it's just stiff from driving. You want me to be in dancing shape for tomorrow, right?"

Matt relaxes, his boyish grin back. "Yes! Good! Okay! I'll let you two get back to..." he snaps, making awkward finger guns, "what it was you were doing. And I'll see you tomorrow! For the wedding! Save me a dance, yeah?"

I nod.

"You, too, Eris! Hope you can dance in those heels!" Matt backs away, finger guns still blazing as he disappears around the corner to the bar.

"Are we sure he's straight?" Eris asks quietly. "He uses a lot of finger guns."

I chuckle. "I mean, he didn't exactly have an identity crisis when I told him I was non-binary. He's just Matt."

"So," Eris turns to me, and my heart thumps in anticipation. Zis lipgloss is sticky on my cheek, and I want it everywhere. "Where should we eat?"

"What?" That's not making out against the wall.

Zis grin is smug. "We were gonna have dinner here. And now we're not. So, townie, where do we eat?"

"I thought..."

Eris's eyebrow raises again. "You thought what, Bambi?" Ze waits, but I just shrug. "You thought I was going to drag you back to the hotel and fuck you within an inch of your life?"

Biting my lip, I shrug again, heat blooming throughout my body. "Kinda."

Ze smirks, stepping closer to me. "Or did you want me to do it here, where anyone might find us? You want Matt to walk by and see you on your knees? You want Allie to hear you scream my name when you come?"

I squirm, shoulders curling around myself. "Well, not *them* specifically, but..."

Eris laughs, and for a second I panic, wondering if I misread this. If ze doesn't want me after all, and that kiss on the cheek was a performance for Matt.

But then Eris strokes my cheek again, right where ze kissed me. The spray of rainbow star freckles curves up as ze smiles, both so close and too far from my lips. "Oh Bambi, I love how needy you are. But be a good little toy and have some dinner first. You'll need your energy."

My head hits the brick with a hard thump as I melt again, and every thought becomes static. That glimmer of euphoria and desire liquefies me into a puddle as Eris pulls me out of the alley by the wrist.

Eleven

FINALLY

Before today, I considered myself a patient person. Someone who played the long game, and explored the options before jumping to a decision. Someone who would wait for the right moment before making my move.

No longer.

Not only did Eris linger over our leisurely dinner of pizza and wine (flirting and teasing me with footsie under the table, while I barely kept my composure), but ze insisted I shower the second we were back, pressing me against the bathroom door and murmuring, "Take some space to think this through. Think about what you want, how far you want this to go, what I can do to make this good for you."

I've never showered quicker in my damn life.

Maybe I should have more whiplash considering two weeks ago, Eris was the most annoying person alive. But I don't. My eagerness surpasses any reservation. I don't care what Eris and I do, I just want to do it. There's a sense of surety with each rushed movement to finish up in the bathroom, an undercurrent of *finally finally finally* pounding in my veins that I should find more confusing than I do.

Mere hours ago, we were dancing around each other. While Eris showered, I raced to change before the water turned off. We didn't acknowledge the shift between us after the car ride. Eris only reconfirmed the limits of affection we agreed on: physical touch and holding hands, flirting, and quick pecks if the situation called for a kiss.

What happened against the wall earlier was within those boundaries, technically. But we never discussed what might happen behind closed doors—I never considered that an option until an hour ago, when the comforting grip of Eris's hands and no-nonsense honesty brought me back to myself. I'm relieved we didn't limit ourselves, because now I want everything.

With no answers to zis questions or my own, I slip a tank top and boxers on my still-damp body, unwrapping my curls from the shower cap as I step out with a cloud of steam.

Adorned in a red silk tank top and shorts with zis long hair loose, Eris is waiting on the bed I claimed when we settled in earlier. Ze pats the duvet next to zim. "Come here."

With a heavy swallow, I lie on my side, hoping I don't look as ungainly as I feel climbing onto the bed. Unsure what to do—because I've only ever done this with Matt before, and all my attempts at a rebound never made it past a kiss—I wait. With Matt, sex was as easy and natural as breathing. With Eris, I'm breathless and trembling.

Eris's eyes trace my body, lingering on the scars that line and twist along my right leg from the thigh down my shin, almost to my ankles. "What's up with your knee?"

"That's not a good foreplay story," I quip.

Eris grins. "Tell it anyway. I'm curious what got your himbo ex so worked up about it that he still feels entitled to tell you what shoes to wear."

I groan, impatient. "It was the summer after eighth grade. We weren't supposed to bike on the highway, but he wanted to go swimming. A delivery driver got distracted, lost control, and pinned me by my leg against a tree. I'm lucky to be alive and still have a leg, but the dairy company the guy worked for paid out enough money to put me through law school."

"Is that why you don't eat dairy?" Eris teases. Zis calloused fingers trace the scars on my knee, numb except where some nerves have regrown.

"No, I'm just lactose intolerant," I snort. "Anyway, I started high school in a wheelchair, and I used crutches or canes until senior year. If it weren't for Matt, I probably would have been bullied to hell for being a nerd, goth, stoner, cripple, the list goes on. But he was super popular, so being his girlfriend protected me from the worst of it. Which is why he's a fucking mother hen now. He blames himself for the accident, so he basically appointed himself as my protector and physical therapist."

"I'm sorry, you were *goth*?" Eris grins in delight.

"That's what you got out of that?" I laugh. "No, I just wore a lot of black. That's basically goth in Solberg. I wouldn't call myself a cripple either, but everyone in school did." I sigh, wondering how we ended up discussing my complicated relationship with being disabled instead of fucking. But Eris wants to hear feelings, so… "The hardest part was losing my independence. I was always such a tomboy—in hindsight, maybe a sign I wasn't cis—and my dad is disabled, with cerebral palsy. So growing up, I always got to do the 'boy' things like mow the lawn and fix the chicken coop, all the stuff that he had trouble doing. He always supervised."

I laugh softly because my dad wasn't a good supervisor either. He always got distracted by the bird feeders. "And after the accident, *Matt* did all of those things. And I had to watch him be my dad's son, while my mom pushed me into being her daughter. Which she'd been doing since I started middle school anyways, telling me it was time to grow up and stop running around without a bra." I chuckle, a little sardonic. "Except it was worse, because Mom treated me like I was helpless and fragile, all while pushing me to be more feminine. I don't think she meant to infantilize me, because she doesn't with my dad, but she did. So did my dad, and the rest of Solberg, even Matt in some ways. I think I'm more bitter about that than being unable to walk for the first year of high school."

Eris nods, humming in acknowledgment. Thankfully, ze doesn't ask anything else, though I do wonder what lies behind zis thoughtful expression. Kneeling on the bed, ze picks up my leg, bending and flexing it with zis hands. My pale skin dips under zis fingers, and a quiet buzz of pain radiates up my thigh. "Does this hurt?"

"Little bit," I admit. "I do stretches and strength training, but I've fallen out of the habit with school. I only do them when the pain is bad."

With another quiet nod, Eris stretches and pushes my leg until I'm rolled onto my back. Zis doe eyes examine my knee, occasionally flicking up to check for my reaction. "So this hurts, but you're not stopping me."

I shake my head. "The pain is there anyway. I'm used to it."

Eris scowls, getting off the bed to dig through zis bag. "There you go, being a doormat again."

"I'm not being a doormat. I just…" Annoyance flashes through me. "You don't have to be so careful with me!"

"No, Blake, I do. But not the way you think." Eris returns with a jar full of yellow gel, kneeling between my legs. "Just some CBD." Ze takes the ankle of my injured leg and rests my foot on zis shoulder. "I won't baby your knee, but you're so…obedient. And I love that, Bambi, I *really* do. I want to make you do all sorts of filthy things for me." Ze unscrews the jar and dips two fingers into the goo, wiping it on my knee before using both hands to spread it up and down my leg.

"Like what?" My belly pools with heat as ze stares at me, hands working the gel into my skin, massaging the scar tissue.

Eris smirks as zis fingertips press deep into the tight muscles of my thigh and calf. "I want you bent over on your knees, begging for me to fuck you. To call you my little slut, and slap that fat ass of yours until it's red and raw and hurts like hell to sit in a church pew tomorrow. But I need to know that you want that. I need to trust that you'll tell me when you don't like something, or when something hurts in a way you don't want. I need you to tell me when you like what I'm doing to you."

I nod, growing wetter by the second, relieved we're back on track. The anticipation is killing me. "I can do that."

"Then tell me, Bambi," Eris kisses my ankle, hand skimming up my legs to pull my hips tight against zim. I can feel how hard ze is through the thin fabric of our shorts, right where I want zim. "What do you want?"

"Kiss me?" My breath is so shallow, it comes out hesitant.

"Trust me, Bambi, that's just the start," Eris smirks. "And then?"

I gape in confusion. Maybe I should have thought about this more in the shower, but I want to do all of the things Eris said and more. "I want everything."

"What's everything?" Eris challenges, crawling over me. My leg folds over zis shoulder and my hips rise to meet zis. "Should I take you like this, all sweet and vanilla, kissing when we come? Or fuck you on your knees with your screams muffled by the pillow?" That gravelly voice is husky in my ear, making me shiver. "You want pain with your pleasure, or do you want me to worship you and drown in your pussy?"

Like stepping in cold water with socked feet, that word dims my buzzing euphoria. "Not that word, but yes to everything else."

Eris beams, rewarding me with a roll of zis hips between my thighs, sending shockwaves through my body. "Good Bambi, tell me what you want me to call this."

I shake my head, unsure of how to answer. "It's just...just a hole. Or cunt. Clit is fine."

"Just a hole, huh?" Eris raises an eyebrow. "Like the good toy you are. Anything else you want me to know? Anything you like to be called, or a way you want me to touch you?"

A glow warms my chest and I fight a smile; this self-proclaimed asshole is being so careful with me. "Try not to cup my chest, but yes. Touch me there. Everywhere."

Eris's hand slides under my tank top, thumb circling my nipple and fingers splayed across my sternum. "Like this?"

I nod, arching into zis touch, still in disbelief that this is happening, that I want this, *need* Eris as much as I do. "Or harder."

With a grin, Eris pinches it, and a grunt escapes me. My thighs clench around zim.

"Tell me what you like," I manage to say through my gasps of pleasure as Eris's rough hands scrape blissfully against my chest. "What should I know?"

Eris's voice is low and close to my ear when ze murmurs, "Do anything you want to my body, call it whatever you want, cock or dick or strap or whatever makes you comfortable. Just don't call me sir, or daddy, or mistress, or any of that. My name is Eris, and I want you to use it." Zis lips catch my earlobe, sucking it into between zis teeth. "Oh, I want you to *scream* it for me, Bambi. You have no idea how much I love hearing you say my name."

"Eris? Can you kiss me now?" I ask, adding a whimpered "please" for good measure.

Eris groans into my ear. "Fuck, you're killing me. You still need to tell me what you want. How you want me."

"Just use me," I whisper, rocking my hips harder against zim, chasing my pleasure and zis. "However you want me, I want all of it. Pain and pleasure and worshiping and all." My voice cracks, and I can't help but babble, "I'll be so good for you, please Eris. Just tell me what you want, and I'll do it. Whatever it is, I'll love it, just make me yours—"

My begging is cut short by a snarl and a bruising kiss, lips crushing against mine—*finally finally finally...* Eris's tongue presses against mine in deep strokes that set the pace for our bodies grinding together. The wine that we had with dinner is on zis tongue, and the sharp edge of zis mustache scratches my lip.

I want more of zim, all of Eris in and around and crushing me. Burying my hands in that silky brown hair that smells like orange zest and gasoline and grass, I twist my fingers around it so we can never be untangled. Eris swallows my moans and lets me drink zis as I pull zim closer.

Too soon, Eris leans back to strip me of my tank top. Zis mouth finds my neck, zis hands teasing at my chest, nails biting into the skin. "Can I leave marks?"

"Please," I gasp, burying my nose in zis hair. I trace the shell of zis ear with my tongue and teeth, gentle around the studs lining the cartilage.

"Someone might see them tomorrow," Eris sucks hard on my pulse anyway. My skin blooms hot under zis teeth.

"Good." I don't care what anyone might think. Right now, I belong to Eris, and I want everyone to know that ze is mine.

Eris's mouth burns down my body, stopping at my nipples. Zis tongue piercing adds a roughness to the teasing licks that leave me squirming and begging for more.

"So fucking needy, Bambi," Eris teases when I lift my hips as zis fingers hook around the waistband of my boxers. Ze slides them off my legs, kissing and biting the skin of my thighs. To my relief, Eris wastes no time stroking me with two fingers, making me gasp with every brush against my clit. "Fuck, you're so wet."

"Well yeah, *someone's* been teasing me for hours." My heart pounds in my throat as Eris sticks zis fingers, shiny and wet and covered in me, into zis mouth.

Eris's eyes flutter shut. "You taste amazing." Ze shoves them roughly inside without preamble, stroking my hole until I'm bucking underneath zim, trying to find purchase for my clit against zis palm. "Taste this," ze pulls zis fingers out and shoves them in my mouth, pressing down on my tongue.

I suck them, moaning as the earthy, sweet taste of me coats my lips and tongue. I grip zis thick forearm with both hands to keep zis fingers in my mouth. The hair coating zis skin prickles my palms.

"Such an eager little slut, sucking on yourself." Eris's other hand slips into me, stroking in time with the fingers in my mouth. My hips roll desperately as I moan, and Eris watches me fuck myself on zis hand with open fascination.

Zis fingers drag from my lips and down my arm to lace our fingers together, as Eris bends down to get zis mouth on me. That tight grip is exactly what I need to hold on for dear life when that tongue ring brushes hard on my clit.

I arch off the bed with a cry. Squeezing zis hand, I bury the other in zis hair to pull Eris where I want zim. Eris groans, dragging zis tongue against my clit so slowly, over and over and over, like ze's savoring every moment. Every lap and lick, kiss and nibble is sensational, but unhurried, and I'm impatient.

Bucking against zis face, I chase the exhilaration climbing up my spine and shooting down to my toes as they curl into Eris' broad shoulders. Despite my babbling, the fruitless pleas for more and faster and *please please please*, Eris keeps a measured pace. Pressure builds through my body, ecstasy mounting inch by excruciating inch, until *finally finally finally*, I shatter under zis mouth.

"You're doing wonderful things for my ego, Bambi," Eris teases, kissing back up my trembling body. "God, you're so responsive. I was worried I wouldn't know if you liked it, and here you are, begging me for more."

"I'd rather be doing wonderful things to your cock," I reply, sliding my hand down the silk of zis camisole.

Eris catches my hand before I can stroke zim through zis shorts. "Trust me, you are. But my plans for you will be cut short if you start touching me now."

I pout, but Eris kisses me, and any thoughts beyond zis mouth on mine—the taste of me coating zis lips, the sweet smell of my arousal soaking zis mustache—are lost.

"I want you on your knees, Bambi," ze murmurs against my mouth.

"You have to get off me," I reply, biting zis lower lip and trapping Eris with my legs around zis hips. The silk of zis shorts, hard and hot through the fabric against my soaking hole, makes us both moan. "And probably get a towel."

Eris beams. "A towel?"

My cheeks burn. "If we're gonna do this from behind, there is a possibility that things will be...gushy."

Zis brow furrows as Eris's smile darkens with delight. "Let me get this straight. You squirt when someone's railing you from behind, and that himbo ex of yours still preferred fucking *missionary*?"

I huff, defensive of Matt even as his protective sweetness smothered me. "As a reminder, he is still haunted by the memory of my leg crushed between a truck and a tree. So yeah, I was not often on my knees."

"I am *so* glad I put the CBD on you now," Eris mutters, pulling away to stomp to the bathroom, yanking zis camisole off to give me a view of zis broad back covered in a stunning willow tree tattoo. "Get on your fucking knees, Bambi."

I try to turn over, but my legs are jelly after coming so hard. I'm still scrambling into position when Eris returns with the towel.

"Oh my god, the fucking snail..." Eris laughs, the cackle sharp. "Never mind, *this* is why he liked missionary."

"Hey!" I sit up, glaring at zim over my shoulder. "At least my snail is cool. Yours looks like a child drew it."

"It's a beautiful tattoo. Very, uh...realistic," Eris says, still chuckling as ze tucks the towel beneath me. As ze touches my lower back, ze cackles loudly again, making me grin along with zim. "This is the funniest shit I've ever seen someone get tattooed there, and I've done a lot of weird tramp stamps."

"What do you have there?" I ask, arching into zis touch as a warm hand drags up and down along my spine. "Or does the tree have roots?"

"Boring, but the tree has roots," Eris kisses my shoulder, zis stubble scraping the skin of my neck. "The best one I ever tattooed was an open mouth, as a target for someone's cum after they pull out. I'd rather cum on your snail, though. Way funnier!"

I swallow hard as Eris fusses with a condom. Zis hand presses between my shoulder blades, guiding me to bend down until my face is pressed into the pillows. I watch over my shoulder as Eris pushes zis shorts off, fisting zis erection before rolling the condom over it. Both of zis nipples are pierced and tattooed into purple heart shapes. I need to know what sounds Eris makes when I suck on them. What that coating of chest and belly hair feels like under my hands. Touch the dozens of tattoos and ask why ze got each one.

Eris smirks when ze notices me watching, slowing zis strokes. "Eager for this, Bambi?"

I nod.

Ze slaps my ass, sharp and hot. I yelp in surprise, moaning when ze does it again to the other cheek. "You like that?"

I nod again, arching my back in a silent question for more; Eris obliges with a few more cracks of zis palm against my ass, until I'm begging zim to fuck me. It's been a long time since anyone else has touched me, and nothing has ever felt half as good as Eris's hard, scorching strikes. My hole is aching to be touched, filled, fucked, anything ze wants.

Eris's hand slides down my arms one by one to pull them behind me, pinning my wrists below my shoulder blades with one hand. Back forced into a deep arch, I'm crushed face-first into the pillow. Delighted and breathless by the weight of zim holding me immobile, I'm at zis mercy, trembling in anticipation.

"Tell me." The head of zis cock slides along my hole, grinding all the way to my clit and back, teasing me. "What do you want?"

I babble a "Fuck me, Eris, please, please, please," into the pillow. My whimper is muffled as ze slowly pushes in, filling me perfectly. Zis gravelly voice echoes through the room in a ragged groan. Eris's hand grips my wrists painfully tight. I can barely move in this position, barely breathe.

I love every second of it.

Eris grasps at my hip to pound into me, zis pace slow but relentless. "Jesus, Bambi, this hole was made for me. You feel so fucking good."

Zis hand on my hip is the only thing keeping me upright. Pleasure climbs up my spine with every thrust. My legs quiver, on the verge of giving out. Eris lets me collapse into the bed, straddling my thighs as ze loops an arm under my hips to keep them angled perfectly and—

"Oh my god," I moan. This is even better. The head of zis cock slides across a spot that drives me wild, each thrust pulling a loud cry from my lips. It's been so long since I've felt this alive and held and needed this way, needed anyone the way I need Eris. "I'm so close, please, don't stop," I sob into the pillow.

"Fuck, you're gonna come from this?" Eris's breath is ragged. "My perfect little hole. You don't even need me to touch your clit, do you?"

"No, need you just like this." That voice, those words, this pressure building down my spine with every thrust. "Please, Eris."

"God, Bambi, I'm coming as soon as you do. You're so fucking gorgeous, begging me for it," Eris says, zis voice strained.

I pant, my thighs quivering as my toes cramp and my back aches. The pain is exquisite. "Please don't stop."

"Say my name again when you come."

I shout, muffled by the pillow, turning zis name and the needy babbling into a prayer as my orgasm surges through me. My body burns white hot as pleasure finally floods all of my senses and my head explodes into blissful white noise.

"That's my Bambi, fucking Christ you're amazing," Eris lets go of my wrists as ze bends over me to finish zimself off, fucking my hole like I'm a toy. Zis body is slick with sweat, and zis chest hair prickles my skin.

I should feel objectified laying here, being used—or perhaps grossed out by the sweat—but I love it. I want more of it, the stretch of each thrust, the weight on my back. I never want zim to stop. Finding Eris's hand as it helplessly grasps at the duvet, I bring it to my lips. Sucking zis fingers, the ones that still smell and taste like me, deep into my mouth, I swirl my tongue around each digit.

It's not enough to bring zim the same incandescent bliss ze showed me, but it's enough to make zim come. Eris's lips press against my spine, cursing under zis breath and hips stuttering until ze slowly collapses over me. Crushing me into the bed once more, Eris is all sweaty hair and heavy breathing like ze ran a marathon, and I preen at how undone I've made zim.

Ze rolls off of me far too soon with a groaned, "Fuck..."

"That good?" I tease to hide the pang of loss, the cooling of my skin in zis absence.

Eris laughs, stretching across the mattress. "Yeah, but I was gonna pull out and come on the snail."

I laugh with zim, turning on my side and wincing as my hip lands in a puddle of damp duvet. "Oh, no!"

"What?"

"We missed the towel."

Eris grins proudly, a manic glint in zis eye. "There's another bed. We'll use that one for sleeping after I've tired you out."

I smile, relieved that this isn't a one-off for Eris either. Crawling over zim to find a dry spot, I let Eris catch me around the waist to pull me on top of zim. Hand dragging up and down my back, ze holds me close as we both catch our breath.

The quiet brings questions that buzz like mosquitos: What does Eris want? How does this change things for us? What happens now?

But just as I start to spiral, Eris kisses me again, silencing my brain with bliss.

Twelve

Jitters

All of my tentative plans for the morning before the wedding—a walk through the wetlands, studying for the bar—are a lost cause. It's midmorning when I blink awake with a smile, wrapped up in Eris. Like a koala, ze clings to my back, snoring into my hair. Though still exhausted from our late night (we didn't climb into the undefiled bed until long after midnight; I lost count of how many rounds because they all blurred together), there's a few hours to spare before we should get ready for the ceremony. I wake Eris with my lips on zis neck, and we use them with languid, sleepy pleasure.

Eris and I don't talk about anything—what it all means, or what ze wants after this trip. Talking now might put a damper on the rest of the weekend, and I want to enjoy whatever it is we've found here instead of overthinking.

Sigurdsson's campus is lovely in summer, smelling of sun-warmed cut grass. The dignified stone buildings are quiet, slumbering giants without the hustle of students flowing through them. Eris looks lovely, if a little tame, in a green cowl-neck dress. Zis heels click against the pavement as we walk towards the chapel.

Along the way, I point out all of my favorite spots, like the bench under an old oak tree where Allie and I used to sit for hours, drinking tea and making up stories about the other students.

Allie and I are very similar, both so desperate to fit in that we hide our inner selves. We clicked right away as roommates, but after that first awkward week of sizing up our fellow freshmen, she turned to me while we sat under that tree. Her shit-eating grin hidden under a sweet smile, she asked, "If I say something really bitchy, do you promise you won't judge me?"

After that, we were bonded eternally. For her, as best friends. For me, also best friends, but one I pined over for years. Other than Matt, no one had ever appreciated my inner pettiness before.

As Eris and I walk across the quad at Sigurdsson, hand in hand, I can tell something is up. The energy of the wedding-goers is off; the quick glances everyone exchanges are eager for gossip. Jessica sees us but doesn't approach, her sour expression heavy with suspicion. Mrs. Jacobson looks frantic, her fake smile frayed as she whispers with the best man, one of Matt's cousins. After how loud Eris and I were last night, I hoped her reaction would be entertaining, but she's too stressed to register my presence.

"What's wrong?" I ask Mr. Jacobson, quick to hide his flask until he recognizes me.

Turning scarlet (making me burn with embarrassment, because I didn't take *his* neighboring presence last night into consideration), he takes another quick pull before putting it away. Matt's father and I have never been friendly, but he's never been as directly antagonistic as Mrs. Jacobson. I think he always hoped I would just quietly disappear. "Matt hasn't been seen in a while," he mutters. "Know anything about that?"

I shake my head, tightening my hand around Eris's. "Haven't heard from him since we left last night. Did he say where he was going?"

Mr. Jacobson shakes his head. "Said he was going to see Allie after the groom's side photos were done, but he never made it to the bridal suite."

Oh, Matt... He was acting strange yesterday, but I never imagined he would disappear from his own wedding, from *Allie*. I squeeze Eris's hand to keep from wringing mine. "Where's Allie? Is she okay?"

"She locked herself into the bridal suite once the bridal party photos were done, and hasn't let anyone in." Mr. Jacobson shrugs, gesturing toward the chapel basement. "I'm just staying out of the way."

I drag Eris along behind me, anxious for my friends and desperate to reassure Allie that I have nothing to do with this. She might not believe me, especially after what her sister said last night, but I have to try.

I knock on the door that bears the bride's name on a pink sign, surrounded by pink flowers. "Allie? It's me. Can I come in?"

"Is there anyone with you?" comes Allie's soft voice.

"It's just me and Eris."

The door unlocks surprisingly quickly. Allie, bundled in a white bathrobe, waves us into a classroom-turned-lounge. The skirt of her poofy princess wedding dress hangs in one corner. "Hurry up, before anyone else sees. Lock the door!"

"Are you okay? What's going on?" I ask, pulling her into a hug. "You took your dress off?"

Eris locks the door behind zim, hanging back.

"Yeah, I'm great! That thing is just impossible to sit down in, so I just took the skirt off." Allie ruffles my hair. "You're such a worrywart!"

I tsk, sounding scarily like my mother. "Then why are you locking everyone else out? Where's Matt?"

Allie snorts. "Oh, Matt is just giving me an excuse to be alone, so I can recharge before the ceremony. I'm so over having a wedding, and tired of smiling, and everyone fussing over me. We should have eloped!"

My groan makes Eris and Allie laugh. "Seriously? Everyone is panicking, and you intentionally caused all this drama?"

Allie shrugs, pouring out two glasses of champagne. "Everyone else has been causing *us* drama for months." She hands one to Eris. "Eris, do you mind hanging out with me? I need to talk about something other than getting married, and I want to hear all about you."

"Uh... Just Eris? What about me?" I ask.

"You, darling? You bring that to Matt," Allie puts another open champagne bottle in my hand. "He said you'd know where he is, and he wants to have a real conversation with you without his mom breathing down his neck. I'd be right there with you, but if I leave this room, I leave the quiet, and if one more person touches me right now, I will scream!"

While Allie makes herself comfortable on the couch, I exchange a look with Eris. "Do you mind?"

"Go for it." Ze nods before turning to Allie with a smirk, finally stepping into the room to join Allie on the sofa. "Suelta el chisme on this bitch."

Allie's responding giggle is angelic, musical and wholly deceptive. "Te diré todo."

"I don't like this," I mutter, letting myself out of the bridal suite. Ignoring the crowd upstairs, I slip out a side door to head towards the woods.

Matt was right; I do know where he is. It was our spot when I lived in the dorms. After finishing up on whatever job site his parents had him working at, he'd come visit me. There's a nature preserve on campus, and we'd hunker down in the duck blind. Get high, fool around, and catch up with each other since we no longer lived next door.

Matt isn't surprised to see me when I duck under the roof; he gives me a nod in greeting as I crouch to climb down into the blind. The air is humid and dank, like wet leaves and weed, despite how airy the wooden observation hut is. The reed-covered windows, paned with spiderwebs instead of glass, overlook the pond.

"Your suit is going to be filthy." I hand him the bottle and sit next to him, not bothering to protect my own black three-piece suit from the grime.

He takes it, trading me for a lit joint, which explains the weed smell. "So's yours. You look good, though."

"Don't let your mom hear you say that," I tease, smoothing my vest down. "You good?"

Matt nods, taking a deep swig of the champagne. "Never better."

"Really? Because you're hiding in a duck blind with your ex, an hour before you're supposed to get married, chugging champagne and smoking...something." I take a puff. It's familiar, but I can't place the strain. "Pretty sure those are all red flags."

"Just CBD. For the nerves." Matt shrugs, taking another guzzle from the bottle, while I take a deeper hit on the joint to soothe my own anxiety. It's got more skunk to it than CBD should have, but maybe I'm just a snob. He lets out a heavy sigh. "Blake, are you happy?"

I cough, panic shooting through me at the implication. "Dude, if there is any question you should *not* ask your ex an hour before your wedding, it's that one."

Matt smacks my arm and steals the joint back. "You're not my ex."

"I am *definitely* your ex."

"Okay, you're not *just* my ex." He takes a quick drag. "You're also my best friend, whom I love and adore eternally."

"Again, weird thing to say to your ex right now, dude." With a laugh, I take a long drink of the champagne, mostly to keep Matt from drinking the whole thing. The bubbles hurt my nose as I chug as much of it as I can. I belch. "Save that for your wife."

"Trust me, Allie knows I love and adore her eternally, too." Matt snorts.

"Are *you* happy?" I ask, already knowing the answer because I know him better than everyone does, except perhaps Allie.

He nods. "When everyone isn't stressing Allie out, yeah. I didn't realize this wedding would be such a big deal for everyone else. I just wanted us to have a good time, not have to manage everyone's egos and hurt feelings."

"Sorry, have you met your mom?" I tease. "I don't know what you expected."

"Yeah, yeah, whatever." Matt rolls his eyes. That boyish grin with the gap between his teeth is as charming as ever. "So yeah, I guess I'm happy. *We're* happy, and we'll be happier once this is all over. I just... I just always thought it'd be you up there with me."

I smack his arm with a dramatic gasp. "Matt! Again, things not to say to your ex!"

"Fuck off, that's not what I meant!" Matt laughs. "I meant as my best man, dipshit. Once things got serious between Allie and me, I knew she was it for me, and I was it for her. It wasn't like that with you and me. You never wanted to get married for one, but I always knew you were meant for more than this place, that you'd never be satisfied with the life that I could offer you. But Allie wants the same things I do."

"What's that?"

"Peace and quiet, mostly," he snickers. "A comfortable, boring life, with good friends and maybe a dog, where our biggest problem is getting our families to respect that we don't want kids," Matt scoffs. "But strangely, the biggest battle we've faced so far has been about you. We had all these jokes that you'd be the ring bearer, or flower child or something, after my mom convinced us that it wouldn't be appropriate for you to be an attendant." He shakes his head, brow furrowed. "But then you never responded to the RSVP, and you stopped messaging us, and we didn't know what to think. Like, we didn't want to lose you, but what if..."

I take Matt's hand. "You won't lose me."

Matt squeezes it. "I wanted to uninvite Jess for that shit she pulled, but you know Allie's soft spot for her."

"I mean, Jessica is her twin," I shrug. "I was just her college roommate."

Matt raises an eyebrow at me. "Yeah, but one of you manipulates all of Allie's insecurities, and the other lets her be herself. Guess who I'd prefer to have around?"

"Giving her room to be herself is your job now, dude." I rest my head on Matt's shoulder, taking a pull from the joint when he holds it up to my lips. "You make everyone feel like everything is gonna be okay, and you need to do that for Allie, too. She internalizes everything, and she needs you to remind her to stop caring so much."

Matt elbows me. "I'm a little offended you think I don't know that. I'm about to be her husband, after all. I'm not that dense."

"I mean, Eris did say you're a himbo."

Matt laughs.

"Though, ze said *I'm* a himbo too, so take that with a grain of salt."

Matt laughs harder, and I laugh with him. The simplicity of it all is a comforting buzz.

"So, you're happy then?" Matt asks. "In Chicago? Being a big-time lawyer and being your gay self out loud and out proud?"

I snort. "I dunno, because I'm not any of that. Not yet, anyway." I pause, and admit quietly, "I haven't been the happiest, but I think I'm getting there."

"I'm sure Eris has something to do with it," Matt grins.

"Can I tell you a secret about Eris?" I ask. Matt nods, and I tell myself to stop talking. But this must be some strong-ass CBD, because I can't stop. "We're not actually together. I brought zim along so you'd think I was happy."

Matt laughs, and I laugh too, because I'm confused why he thinks that me lying to him is so funny. "Bloke, dude, you're so weird. You don't need to be with someone to be happy."

"I know. But also, I didn't want to be the only single person at your wedding." I stare out of the duck blind across the wetlands around us, counting up the mallards and red-winged blackbirds.

He giggles to himself before saying, with far too much gravity, "Well, even if you're not official, you're still cute together. The way Eris looks at you, the way you look at zim, there's something there."

"You think so?" I hope so.

Matt smirks. "Well, that, and the giant ass hickey on your neck that wasn't there yesterday." He prods my throat.

I smack his hand away. "I hope you're right. Eris and I haven't really gotten along before this. But I like zim, and I want to see what happens."

"Good."

I take another deep drag on the joint, now half gone. "Where did you get this?"

"Your parents."

I laugh, and Matt laughs with me, though he has no idea why. I stub it out onto the bench and dig into his pocket for the tube my parents store their homegrown rolls in. "Dude, there is *no* way this is CBD." I grin. "You're gonna be fucking baked for your wedding!"

Matt giggles. "Oh, god, Allie is gonna kill me."

"She's getting drunk with Eris as we speak. But good luck with your vows, man!" I check my phone to see what time it is— "Oh my god!" My background is a picture of my ass with Eris's cum all over the snail. Ze took it this morning, at my request, so I could see what it looked like. "How the fuck did this become my lock screen?"

"Holy shit!" Matt shouts, then cracks up. "Not together, my ass!"

"I am going to kill that fucker! This was *not* my background when we left the hotel!"

While Matt and I crawl out of the duck blind, I text Eris that I'm going to strangle zim. By the time we've dusted each other off, Eris has texted me back a selfie of zim and Allie flicking me off. I make that my background instead.

Matt crouches down in front of me. "Hop on, Bloke. Save your knee for the dancing."

"I can walk. Eris put some CBD on my knee. Like actual CBD, not my parent's homegrown shit." Not that it reduced the pain much, but Eris and Matt don't need to know that.

"From the sound of it, ze put a lot of things on you," Matt teases. "C'mon, let me give you a ride, for old times' sake."

"I should have made a bingo board of things not to say to your ex before you get married," I tease, but I hop on his back anyway. It's Matt's day, after all, and he likes to take care of people. If he wants to take care of me, even though I don't need him to, I'll let him. One last time.

Thirteen

The Wedding

After Matt drops me off back on the quad (fortunately only a few minutes late for the family photos), I find Eris waiting for me on the edges of the gathering crowd of guests. Zis face is hard to read, but ze doesn't seem as open as I've come to expect in the past day.

"Everything okay?" I ask, a curl of anxiety tightening my chest.

Eris nods. "You and Matt must have had a good talk."

I grin, putting my arm around zis waist. "Yeah. Hope Allie wasn't too hard on you."

Ze shakes zis head, not leaning into me the way ze did earlier. "She's funny. Got a dark sense of humor for someone so bubbly."

"What'd she say about me?"

Eris replies in a string of Spanish, none of which I can follow in my inebriated state.

"En Ingles, por favor?"

Eris snorts. "She says you're self-centered and conceited."

"Shut up!" I laugh. "She did not!"

Zis smile doesn't quite reach zis doe eyes, but that's all the reply I get.

"Oh, by the way, I hate you." I elbow zim as we walk into the chapel, where all Siggys are supposed to want to get married. As a born and raised atheist, I haven't been here much, but Allie's parents insisted she get married in the same chapel they did. "Really? My lock screen?"

That at least gets a true grin on Eris's face, but ze only offers up an unabashed shrug.

Catching Eris's hand, I lace my fingers between zis as we follow everyone into the church, finding a pew near the middle. Like any other Minnesotan small town, anyone who isn't family sits as close to the exit as possible, so the back rows are full. "Hey, can you drive us to the reception after?"

Eris leans in to loudly sniff me, examining me in amusement, but still distant. "I dunno. I might get contact high from sitting next to you."

I laugh half-heartedly, my chest tightening. "Well, it's not too far to walk if we need to." I'm not sure if the weed is making me paranoid, but it wasn't that hard to make zim smile this morning. I hate being that person who always thinks everyone is mad at me, but... Is Eris mad at me?

No, it's probably just the weed talking. Eris simply isn't on my level; I've smoked a quarter of Matt's "CBD" and drank most of a bottle of champagne. I wrap an arm around zis shoulders, wincing as I try to get comfortable on the hard wooden pew after last night. A reminder that even if Eris is acting reserved now, ze was desperate for me last night.

The wedding is beautiful. Matt and Allie cry and laugh together as they exchange their vows and rings and kiss, their visible anxiety endearing. The two of them are blissfully perfect, like I knew they would be, the way I've been dreaming about since freshman year.

For as long as I had deluded myself into thinking I belonged with them, I'm where I'm supposed to be today: Watching them with love and support in my heart, and then returning to my new life, decidedly larger and louder than the quiet one they want to build together. More stressful and more free, and just *more*. A place where all of me fits, instead of being constrained by social norms I never understood and could never follow, because I wasn't meant to.

Hopefully, Eris wants to be part of that place, too.

AT THE RECEPTION, WE stay unobtrusive, though Jessica looks like she might slip arsenic in my drink if she gets too close. I ignore her, focusing on Eris, who still seems closed off. However, ze quietly talks shit in my ear and clings to my hand enough to reassure me that I'm overthinking everything. Zis presence keeps me grounded during dinner when, thankfully, we're seated with old acquaintances from Sigurdsson who knew me as Allie's roommate or Professor Ryan's kid, not as Matt's ex. The Jacobsens avoid us like the plague, though Allie's parents' greeting is polite (though brief).

After the first dance, Jessica finally works up her courage. She corners me as I exit a bathroom stall (I prefer the women's because it's generally cleaner, and I know the rules there). "You have some nerve. If I were you, I wouldn't have even come to the ceremony, and yet here you are, still showing your face at the reception. Shameless."

"I don't know what you're talking about." I must still be a little high, because the water makes my hands tingle as I wash my hands, and I can't come up with a better response.

"You disappear with the groom before the wedding, get him drunk, and come back with a hickey on your neck and hanging all over him."

I frown, but force myself to pause. I can see how that might look bad. "Look, my best friend had some pre-wedding jitters. I was there for *platonic* moral support," I reply without looking at her; I'm already irritated by her implication without the sight of her pinched expression. "Allie handed me the bottle herself and told me to bring it to him. If *she* trusts me, why are you so paranoid?"

"My sister matters more to me than anyone in the world," Jessica hisses, edging closer as I dry my hands on the towel. "She needs someone to have her back because she's too blind to think you would ever do anything wrong—"

"Jess." Allie opens the handicap stall with a bang, hauling her giant poofy skirt through the stall door. "Shut up."

"You were supposed to tell me when you needed the bathroom!" Jessica whines, rushing over to fluff Allie's already fluffy skirt. "That's my job!"

"I can piss like a big girl all by myself. The detachable skirt is the whole reason I agreed to get this obnoxious cupcake dress!" Allie exchanges a deadpan look with me as she washes her hands. "Enough. Leave Blake alone."

"But she—"

"*They* are my good friend, who both Matt and I want at our wedding. They came here to support us, not to get harassed by you! I don't need you to stand up for me, or fight battles I don't want fought." Allie dries her hands and throws the towel in the bin, putting her hands on her hips. "I didn't ask you to be my maid of honor to help me use the bathroom, or to make sure my best friend doesn't seduce my husband, or to make executive decisions about who to invite to my wedding. You're my maid of honor because I trusted that my twin would put me first. And yet, everything is fucking pink! My favorite color is seafoam green!"

Jessica blinks, silent.

I'm left equally speechless. I've never seen Allie so assertive towards anyone before, especially not Jessica. After her silence yesterday, I was worried that Allie thought Jessica was right. A sigh of relief escapes me. She wasn't mulling over her feelings about me at all, just her bitchy twin.

"I asked you to leave Blake and Eris alone today, and you can't even do that. Maybe I should have asked them to be my attendant of honor instead, if this is how you behave!" Allie grabs my hand. "Come on, Blake. Let's dance."

She pulls me out of the bathroom with more force than necessary, because I'm dogging her every step. "You okay?"

Allie nods. Her cheeks are flushed, a determined smirk on her face. "I feel great! That's been building for months, and Eris helped me figure out what I wanted to say. God, champagne is amazing!"

"Proud of you," I say, and Allie beams up at me, batting those big blue eyes. When we lived together, that grin would send my heart to my toes before twisting into endless heartburn from the guilt of being in love with someone other than Matt. But now, that grin merely gives me a nice buzz, a pleasant high from being home with my best friends. "But you know I would have been a terrible attendant of honor."

"Oh yeah, without question!" Allie giggles, fussing with her princess skirt. "You should've been Matt's best man, though. I'm sorry that you're not." Her grin turns mischievous. "My new mother-in-law isn't ready. If there's one thing I've learned from this wedding bullshit, it's that I need to keep *my* peace, not hers."

We laugh as Allie grabs my hands to pull me onto the dance floor. In the corner table, I see Eris sitting by zimself, and my chest tightens. But before I can beckon zim over, Matt pounces on zim with a hug from behind, dragging zim to join us. Eris's dress flutters around zis stocky legs as Matt spins zim around the mostly empty space (it's cute that they thought anyone from Solberg would dance at a wedding). Eris's flustered expression makes me smile, knowing ze's caught in the throes of Matt's charm.

"You're staring," Allie teases me.

I shrug, unashamed. I'm allowed to stare at this point. I hope, anyway.

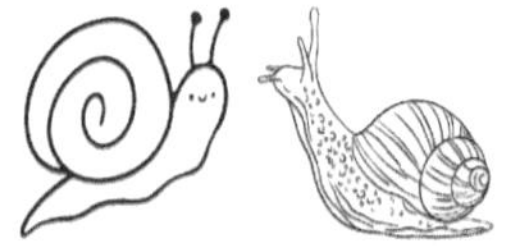

As my high wears off, and the sleepiness from champagne settles in, it becomes more apparent that Eris is avoiding me. Not necessarily physically. Ze sits close enough to touch, brings me a much-needed cup of coffee while I get us cake; all the things a real couple would do. But ze has barely looked at me all evening. After last night, I thought we'd turned a corner in our...friendship, for lack of a better word. But Eris hasn't talked shit about me, or made a dirty joke too loudly, or laughed with that high-pitched cackle since we arrived on campus.

Ze hasn't called me Bambi in hours.

"Are you mad at me?" I ask quietly as we finish our cake, hating how weak my voice sounds. "Did I do something wrong?"

Eris frowns, shaking zis head. "No, of course not."

"Then what's wrong?"

Ze shrugs. "Nothing."

I wait, in case Eris wants to add anything. Maybe ze isn't feeling well, maybe Jessica said something that struck home, or maybe the heteronormativity is giving zim a headache. But Eris just scrapes raspberry drizzle off zis plate and sucks on the fork.

I drain the last of my coffee, setting the cup down with a too-loud *thunk*. "Come on."

Eris looks up at me as I stand, extending my hand in a silent offer. After a reluctant pause that makes my heart sink, considering how ze clung to my hand on the long drive here, ze rises and takes it. "Where are we going?"

"To dance, duh." I don't know what song is playing, but it's slow and sweet. If Eris is already checking out of whatever we are, I want to cling just a little while longer. Even if it is for pretend, I want to feel wanted. To hold zim while we slow dance, and kiss zis cheek.

Eris dutifully put zis arms around my shoulders, zis face in my neck. In a kitten heel, ze fits perfectly in my arms. I draw zim close around the waist, resting my cheek on zis hair. "Who are you, and what have you done with the real Eris?"

"The fuck are you talking about?" Eris huffs.

"You've been quiet. You haven't insulted me in hours. You've been...nice. It's weird."

Zis chuckle is silent, but the exhale is hot against my skin. "You told me not to be an asshole. I'm not being an asshole. You're welcome."

"I never expected you to be *nice*, though. Especially to me," I tease as we sway side to side. The satin of zis dress is smooth under my palms. "What happened to not making yourself small for them?"

"I'm not making myself small," Eris grumbles quietly into my collar. "I'm just...not drawing attention to myself. For you."

"Okay, but we've established that I like you kinda bitchy." I kiss Eris's ear.

Eris sighs, burying into my shoulder. "I just... You're so much more *you* here. I've never seen you this open, or laugh this much. This place, these people—they're important to you. I don't want to ruin things."

"You couldn't," I insist. "I love home, parts of it at least. But nothing you could do would ruin it. I'm here for Matt and Allie, and they like you. My parents won't care what anyone says about us, even if I worry about making things harder for them. Those four are the only ones I care about here. And I... I care about you, Eris."

Eris's distressed grumble makes me grin.

"Seriously, I appreciate you so much. I was so anxious about this weekend, and you've made it all so manageable. Yeah, I'm laughing and I'm having fun here, but a big part of that is because of you." I pause. "And the weed, but mostly you. You're the one who encouraged me to come here, to be brave enough to stand up for myself. You make me laugh, and you make me come so hard I scream," I murmur, my lips tugging into a grin. "You know, Matt's mom hasn't said a word to me yet today, and you deserve full credit for that." Eris snorts into my collar, and I add quietly in zis ear, "And you look gorgeous in that dress tonight, and I'm really looking forward to taking it off of you later."

"Shut the fuck up, Bambi," Eris scowls, cheeks darkening under the dim light of the dance floor. That's all the warning I have before ze kisses me, hard and hot. Zis fingers tangle in the curls on the back of my neck. "Stop being so fucking sweet."

"But you like it."

"Too much." With a glare, ze kisses me again.

"You want to get out of here?" I ask.

Eris's glare falters, biting zis lip and looking away. "Don't you want to spend more time with your friends?"

I glance over to where Matt and Allie are dead on their feet, pretending to dance. Matt is holding her against his chest, letting her hide from everyone demanding too much from her, because that bitch can never say no. "I think they want to leave even more than we do."

Fourteen

There's Only Now

THE MOMENT OUR HOTEL room door swings shut, I shove Eris back against it, kissing zim like I need zim to breathe. Zis tongue against mine tastes of champagne and coffee and chocolate cake and raspberry drizzle as we devour each other. Our kiss is dizzying, both of us breathing through quick gasps and moans as our hips roll together.

Eris's hands fist at my shirt, pulling it from my slacks. Zis nails scrape my bare skin to pull me closer, making me shiver from how eager ze is for me, how desperate we are for each other. "Bambi," ze hisses when I nibble zis lower lip.

"Eris," I murmur, moving to zis neck.

"Fuck, you're..." ze trails off. "God damn it, Blake. Wait."

That's not what I like to hear when I'm leaving a hickey, especially not in such a serious tone. I pull away. "What, what's wrong?"

"We shouldn't do this."

My heart drops, and I step back. "What?"

Eris slumps back against the door, looking at zis feet.

I wait, burning with mortification. Perhaps I've misread something, and Eris actually is mad at me. But ze stays silent. "Talk to me Eris. If I did something wrong, I'm sorry. But can I at least know what I did?"

"It's not you. Allie said—"

"What the fuck did Allie say?" I snap.

"Nothing!" Eris shakes zis head, raking a hand through zis long hair. It's been thoroughly messed up from me already, and seeing zim smooth out the snarls I made hurts. "I just..." Ze groans. "God damn it, I have to talk about feelings and shit! I hate this." Ze pushes off the door and stalks past me, kicking off zis heels. Dress swishing with every stomp, Eris paces around the bed we slept in last night, zis bed technically.

Giving zim space, I sit on the end of the other bed, the one we fucked in, waiting.

"Okay, so here's the deal." Eris bunches zis skirt in zis fists. "I have kind of had a little—well, no not little, but whatever—little thing for you for a while."

I blink, more than confused, because Eris has always been pretty condescending and rude to me. Then again, ze is condescending and rude to everyone. I've always admired how ze can be so enviably unapologetic about it. "How long is a while?"

Eris winces. "Like, since we met."

I choke on my surprise. "Two years?!"

"Yeah. I know. Stella and Dream give me shit for it constantly." Eris sits on the bed we slept in, too far away. "At first, I thought it was just, you know, attraction or whatever. But then you never let me get away with shit like you do with everyone else. Like, you were so nice and sweet to everyone but me, and I thought that was funny."

"You liked that I was a dick to you?" I ask skeptically, not daring to look up, instead staring at the snake tattooed around zis ankle.

Eris scoffs. "Like you're one to talk."

"Fair." I nod for zim to continue, burying my hands under my thighs.

"I never expected you to let me be your plus-one to begin with, and I never expected us to get along so well, or see what you're really like when we're alone, or *anything* that happened last night," Eris digs a toe into the carpet. "You always seemed so lonely back home. But you have these wonderful, weird, straight people who love you so much, and you're letting me see the you that they see, and I am honored that you're letting me in like this." Zis fingers tighten around the duvet cover. "But what if it doesn't last past this weekend? What if we go back to how it was, and you pull away and shut me out?" Ze groans again. "I just... I dunno. My heart's in it now, and I don't think it's a good idea to fool around again when it's one-sided."

My head snaps up to look Eris in the eyes, but ze is staring at zis feet. "Who says it's one-sided?"

Eris huffs. "Blake, you literally could not stand to be around me before yesterday. How is it *not* one-sided? You might like me here and now, but this isn't real. If we were back in Chicago, would you be holding my hand or whispering sweet shit in my ear? No, and I can't let myself forget that. Going back to normal after getting in so deep with you is already gonna suck hard, and I don't want to make it worse."

I sigh, quietly gathering my courage to admit, "You scared me."

Eyes shining, Eris looks at me, confused.

"It's not that I couldn't stand you. You were so confident, and outspoken, and interesting, and yes, attractive." I shake my head, laughing at the memories of how confused and hurt and lost I was two years ago. "But I was just coming out of an eight-year relationship where I knew my ex and the woman I was in love with would get together as soon as I was gone. I didn't have any friends, and I was in a new city after living in the same podunk town my whole life and just starting law school." I wrap my arms around myself. "I couldn't let myself see you as anything other than an annoying acquaintance. You would have derailed my whole plan."

Eris shakes zis head, hair hiding zis face. "And you're about to start a demanding career, so I still don't fit into your plan."

"I don't have a plan anymore!" I fall back on my bed with a frustrated groan. "I take the bar next month, and I'm so overprepared because I haven't let myself do anything *but* study for two fucking years! My whole life, spite has kept me going, but since moving to Chicago, I've just been lonely and anxious and sad. I want to *live* more, Eris, but I don't know how." My voice cracks, but I fight the crushing wave of vulnerability. "You said you were gonna drag me out of my head and make me hang out with everyone, and I want that! I want to spend time with you, to get to know you better. Not just as a friend, but in any way you let me."

I roll onto my side, propping my head up on my elbow. I will Eris to look at me, so ze knows how much I mean it. But ze won't meet my burning eyes. My voice softens as I say, "This can be real, if you want that. I want to hold your hand and tell you how gorgeous you are, and get to know Stella so I can tease you with them. So don't say this is one-sided. I want so much for myself, Eris, and you're at the heart of everything."

Eris sits silently, looking hard at the floor before whispering, "You say that, but what happens when we get back, and it doesn't work out?" Ze runs a hand through zis hair, still not meeting my eyes. "I act confident, but you heard how my mom talks to me, how only my grandma cares if I'm alive, and she doesn't even remember me. That shit cuts deep. I believe that you mean what you're saying now, but how can you know what you'll want later? Letting myself feel more, only to have you reject me when we're back to reality... I'm scared shitless by how hard I've fallen for you in a fucking day!" Eris glances at me, just for a moment, eyes wide and earnest, before ze looks back at the floor with a muttered, "Fuck!"

I sit in silence, searching for the right words to make Eris believe me. But I don't know that I can. The pain in zis voice won't be solved with a conversation, not a hundred conversations. Nothing I say or do tonight will change zis mind. Only trust, slowly built moment by moment, will. My chest aches with the echo of Matt breaking up with me; his mind was made up, too. But with Eris, it's not about me. This time, instead of Matt ending things for my own good, Eris is keeping me away for zis.

I have to respect that.

"Fine," I say, sitting up to pull my stuffy formalwear off. I set my lighter and the tube leftover from my conversation with Matt onto the nightstand, chucking my suit towards the suitcase. Nothing hits the mark, but I can't be bothered to pick any of it up.

In my binder and boxers, I crawl up the bed—my bed now, instead of the bed we fuck in—and flop onto my stomach. I wish it was still filthy with us, but the linens are fresh, as if last night never really happened. Eyes burning, I open my laptop to my bar study guide.

"Blake," Eris sighs. "I didn't mean to piss you off—"

"You didn't," I shoot zim a half-hearted smile over my shoulder, hoping my eyes aren't red. "I like you, Eris, and I want to see where this goes. If you can't believe that tonight, then I won't pressure you. Trust me, I will show you I mean it when we're back home, if that's what you need.

"But," I roll on my side to face zim, "Regardless of what happens, nothing will change how I feel about you right now. So if you want another night together before we return to reality, I am willing and eager to fulfill anything you want from me. Because last night was glorious, *you're* glorious, and I want more." I shrug and turn back to my laptop as my voice wavers. "But that's your call. I'll entertain myself by studying, if that's not what you want."

Eris sits silently for a long time, zis deep breaths the only sound in the room.

I'm about halfway through the case study (which I'm not paying attention to at all, because my head is swirling and my heart aches) when Eris stands. Made delusional by my own desperation, I half expect zim to join me on the bed. To tell me ze changed zis mind and needs me as much as I need zim.

Instead, Eris shuffles around the room. Unzipping the dress I wanted to take off of zim. Brushing zis teeth in the bathroom, instead of kissing me.

Staring blankly at the laptop, I'm overwhelmed by embarrassment and confusion as the minutes tick by. The hot tears welling in my eyes make my screen impossible to read.

"Bambi," Eris murmurs, the bed we slept in—no, *zis* bed—creaking as ze sits on the edge. Too close now, zis gravelly voice too gentle. "Come here."

I shake my head, refusing to look over so ze won't see my hurt. "You wanted space."

"Blake, please."

"I'm doing what you wanted," I snap, my voice cracking. "If you've changed your mind, *you* come here."

A tattooed hand snaps my laptop shut. The "amor" on Eris's knuckles is more discernible than any word on the screen. "Look at me. Please."

"No."

"You're such a brat, Bambi." Eris rolls me onto my back, straddling my waist. Zis weight is heavy and comforting on my hips. "I'm sorry." Those doe eyes gaze softly down at me. Zis thumb strokes my cheek, and it takes everything in me not to lean into Eris's touch. "I just... Thank you for being honest, and giving me space to get my head out of my ass. I'm scared of getting hurt, but I'm going to hurt anyway. At this point, regret would feel worse."

"So you do want me?" The question sounds ridiculous even as I say it, because I know Eris wants me. But the rejection still stung, still *stings*.

"Oh, Bambi, never doubt it," Eris leans down to kiss my cheek, right below my eye, hair tickling my face. "I just... I can't think about what comes after yet. If I let myself hope tonight, it's going to hurt more when things don't go the way I want. Because we're not ourselves here. You're about to start a new job, you've had an emotionally intense weekend, and we're isolated from reality. Everything could change once we're back in Chicago for longer than five seconds."

I huff, a mix of frustration and affection at how easily Eris accepts zis own conflicting feelings. I can't imagine feeling anything other than desperate yearning, now that I've let myself admit I want zim. But if both having me and not having me is what Eris needs, then I can do my best to give zim that. "Okay, when we're back home for longer than five seconds, then. For tonight, no more talk of after," I say, setting my chin defiantly. "But we're still here now."

Eris takes a long look at me before nodding. "We're here now." Ze practically growls in frustration, cupping my jaw tight like ze did last night outside of the bar. "How do you do this to me, Bambi?"

I grip zis wrist, twisting slightly to kiss the pad of zis thumb. "What do you want, Eris?" I ask, sucking zis thumb into my mouth until Eris's cock swells, hot and heavy against my stomach, straining the silk of zis shorts. "If you can only dream about tonight, what happens right now?"

"I want you every way there is to have you." Eris's doe eyes are almost black with desire. Ze kisses my cheek again, murmuring directly into my ear, "I want you to fuck my face until you can't walk, I want you sucking me so deep that you choke, I want you upside down and backward and every which way until you can't even remember your own name, because you're too busy screaming mine."

I whimper, thighs clenching and hips bucking for purchase. But Eris's strength keeps me pressed to the bed.

"But most of all, I want you on your back, kissing me and telling me you're mine when we come." Eris nips my neck then, the same spot where ze left a hickey. "I want you needy and desperate and begging for more. So in case this doesn't work out, I can at least remember what it was like to have you."

"Fuck, Eris, I'm yours." I bury my face in zis neck, inhaling zis grassy musk and the warmth of zis skin. "And you're mine. I'll never let you forget that, so shut up and kiss me already."

With a quiet laugh, Eris cups my face and finally kisses me, hard and eager. Fingers lacing through my hair, ze pulls it to angle our mouths more perfectly together. Zis tongue pushes between my lips to glide against my own in a deep, steady rhythm.

I cup Eris's ass, encouraging zim to hurry up and fuck me again. But Eris takes my hands and pins them to the bed. "Be patient."

Before I can protest, Eris slides down my body, letting my hands up to pull my boxers off. Maybe I am a brat, because my hands fly to zis shoulders, too desperate for contact with zis smooth brown skin to stay where Eris put them. Arching my back, I wrap my legs around zis waist, crying out as ze strokes two fingers deep into my hole. Still sore from last night, every ache is bliss.

Eris smirks, brushing zis thumb against my clit until I'm a writhing, sobbing mess from just zis hand. "How many times will I get you off tonight, Bambi? We got you to five last night. Think you can give me more than that?"

"Yes, please," I beg, gripping zis wrists to pull one of zis hands firmly against my throat, chasing my pleasure with the other. "Please, don't stop."

"Go on, gorgeous." Eris looks down at me in awe, a slow grin spreading across zis face as zis chest heaves, thumb tracing my pulse. "Take what you need."

Toes curling into the meat of zis calves, I cling to Eris. My fingernails bite into zis forearms hard enough to leave marks as I keep zis hands where I'm most vulnerable, exactly where I need. I whimper Eris's name when I come on zis fingers, a needy broken cry escaping zis grip on my throat when my body curls and twists in that most precious agony, because it drives zim wild to hear it.

As soon as I stop twitching, Eris's hand leaves my throat to scramble for a condom on the bedside table. For someone who "never expected" things to end up here, Eris came optimistically prepared with a whole box. I want to tease zim for it, but that might land too sharply after how vulnerable ze's been tonight.

"Bambi, you drive me fucking wild." Eris leans back to strip. Silk falls away from zis body, revealing the round belly and the muscular arms and thighs. The shitty tattoos are a stark contrast with the gorgeous art embedded in zis skin. Nipple rings shine against the purple hearts buried beneath zis chest hair.

Eris strokes zis erection before rolling on the condom, and I drink in the glory of Eris touching zimself. Strikingly beautiful with smudged eyeliner and star-speckled cheekbones, ze looks at me like I'm zis salvation. "You want this off?" Eris asks, tracing the edge of my binder along my ribcage as ze leans in to kiss me.

"No, keep it on." After the whiplash of how hot and cold Eris has been tonight, I feel more grounded within it. "Stop stalling."

Eris laughs into my shoulder, a quieter version of zis piercing cackle. A laugh just for me. "So fucking needy, aren't you?"

"Just for you, Eris," I murmur, nuzzling the studs lining zis ear. Whimpering when ze pushes my knee over zis shoulder to thrust into me, hard and slow and perfect

"God, the sounds you make," Eris rasps as ze fucks me, all teeth and tongue and lips along my neck. I'm going to have more marks on top of the bruises from yesterday. "I love how much you need me."

I can't reply other than a grunt when zis fingers twine through my hair, yanking my head back to suck the underside of my jaw.

"Tell me if I'm too much, okay?"

I shake my head, squeezing zis ass to encourage zim to fuck me faster. "You could never be too much."

Eris groans deep into my ear, hips jerking at my touch. "Promise you will anyway. I don't want to hold back with you, and I need to know you'll stop me if you don't like it."

"Don't hold back, I want all of you."

"Bambi," Eris warns, zis gravelly voice low and promising.

I huff in impatience. "Fine, I promise."

Eris kisses me then, just like ze's fucking me, hard and rough and breathless. Each deliberate, methodical stroke of zis cock hits perfectly, sending shockwaves through my body and moans between our lips. Zis fingers slide down my thigh, calloused fingertips rough as they circle my clit.

"Fuck, you're glorious," Eris says as I arch underneath zim, pleasure coursing through my veins as zis cock and fingers work together to break me. I'm so close, my vision whites out, but it's not enough to bring me over the edge again. "Don't force it, Bambi," Eris mutters against my lips as I whimper in frustration. "You're so impatient. Just breathe through it, that's it."

"You feel so good, please don't stop Eris," I gasp for breath. Tears prickle in my eyes, frustrated that my body isn't cooperating. This should be enough.

"You needy bitch, of course I won't stop," Eris teases. "You're mine, and I'm going to make you come if it kills us."

My laugh sounds more like a sob. But when my body is on the verge of exploding and my skin is so tight it hurts, I may as well be crying.

"Tell me, Bambi," Eris whispers into my ear, sucking on my earlobe. "Tell me you're mine."

"I'm yours, Eris. Only yours."

"Tell me who makes you feel this good."

"You do, please Eris, you feel amazing, please never stop." I'm right on the edge again, on the verge of tipping over. But there's something just out of reach, keeping me from my peak.

"Tell me whose hole this is."

"Mine," I tease, panting and gasping and touching every inch of Eris I can reach. Scrambling for purchase, I scratch welts across zis glowing skin. "But I want you to use the fuck out of it."

Eris laughs, that quiet version that's mine and mine alone, and pinches my clit. "Fucking brat. I should stop just for that."

But I'm already convulsing, crying out Eris's name, mind blank and reeling. That shock of pain bursting through me has finally, *finally* pushed the pleasure coursing through me over the edge. Eris's teeth sink into my bottom lip as ze moans, cursing as zis body shudders with mine, zis thrusts uneven, wild, and deep.

Eris sags against me, breathing ragged. "God, Bambi, you've ruined me for everyone else."

"Good," I catch my breath, boneless and trembling, clinging to Eris with every limb to keep zim close, soothing the lines my nails carved in zis skin. I want to say more, to let spill all of the dreams and plans in my head for us. But ze doesn't want those thoughts of after. Tonight is only for now.

We lay there, quiet and holding each other, until Eris kisses zis way down my body to go down on me in the laziest way—using my thigh as a pillow. Each kiss to my cunt is slow and sweet and perfect. I play with zis hair and tell Eris how pretty ze is while I fuck zis mouth. That fucking tongue piercing makes me come twice more, before I need a break.

When I return from the bathroom, Eris is sitting back against the headboard, looking as wrecked and used as I feel. The window is cracked open to air out the room. I crawl between zis legs, peppering zis body with kisses and wiping the sweat and spit and cum away with a warm washcloth. Eris twitches in my hand, half hard by the time I'm done, so I lay on my stomach between zis legs to return the favor.

Eris watches me with a lazy smile on zis lips while I play with zim, figuring out what makes zim react. Last night, I didn't get a chance to explore like this, to map out where ze likes my hands and tongue. How much ze likes it when I gently slide back the foreskin—which I'm not used to but am fascinated by—running my tongue along zis slit, salty with precum. Exploring how far I can take zim down my throat before I gag. If ze likes when I cup zis balls, or press my knuckles into zis perineum more.

"Look at you, Bambi," Eris whispers, cupping my cheek.

I grin, popping off zis cock with a slurp to press a wet kiss into zis wrist. My feet kick in the air as I suck zim deep and slow, with no urgency or desperation. "After" is forever away, and we have all night.

With a dazed and dreamy smile on zis face, Eris seems in no hurry either. Reaching over to the nightstand, ze passes over the condoms to examine the roach Matt and I shared earlier. "May I?"

I nod with a hum, mouth stuffed full of zim.

Eris opens the tube, sniffing as ze grabs the lighter. "What is this?"

"Homegrown," is the only explanation I can muster without interrupting my task. Better not to talk about my parents right now anyway.

"That could mean anything," Eris teases as ze lights it, taking a deep pull. Smoke billows out around zis septum ring. "Fuck, that's good, though. Want some?"

I nod again, and Eris pulls me off of zim with a fist in my curls, holding the joint between my lips so I can take a drag. I grin at zim as I exhale, licking the head of zis cock as smoke billows out of my mouth.

Eris groans, brown eyes widening. Ze pulls me up the bed with a tug of my hair, sticking the joint between my lips so ze can reach for another condom. "Jesus Christ,

Bambi, and here I thought you were gonna be so uptight, that it'd be fun to unwind you. I knew you'd be a freak, but you're fucking depraved."

With a smug grin, I wait until the condom is on before sinking onto zim, smiling at the ache and stretch of zim. Taking another pull on the joint, I shotgun the smoke into Eris's mouth. "Your freak."

Eris grins. The scars on zis lips pale as zis smile widens. "That's fucking right. My depraved toy."

I kiss zim, slow and patient and sweet, stretched full as I grind on zis cock. Zis mustache is damp, scented with the earthy sweetness of my cunt and the grassy, citrusy smoke. I run my thumbs along those hairs, fingers caressing the stars on zis cheeks. "I want one of these."

"The tattoo freckles or a mustache?" Eris asks. "Because Dream did my freckles."

Our mutual lack of urgency slows my movements until we're no longer fucking, but still intimately entwined. "Both, but I meant the mustache."

"Grow one, then," Eris replies, kissing my thumb. "You'd look like redneck trash with the mullet *and* a pornstache, but I'd still think you're hot."

I laugh. "Maybe I will. I've always wanted to start T."

"Why haven't you?" Eris flicks the lighter on so I can relight the joint, arm wrapping around my hips to hold me in place, quiet and still and full of zim as I smoke. Ze seems just as content as I do to stretch this out. Maybe I have been too impatient, because this is delightful.

"You won't like the answer." I sigh, burying my face into zis collarbone while I tap the ashes into a water cup on the nightstand.

"Is the answer because you're worried about what your parents will think?" I don't respond, and that's enough for Eris. Ze huffs. "Yeah, you're right, I don't like the answer."

"I'm not as bold as you," I murmur. "I don't want to lose them."

"What makes you think they're going anywhere?" Eris asks, warm hand stroking my back. "There's always a risk, but from what you've told me, your parents will come around. You're out to them now, and they're still in your life. Having a raggedy-ass mustache and a voice like a twelve-year-old boy for a while isn't going to change that. Knowing your doormat ass, you haven't brought up your gender again since you came out."

I huff, because I haven't. "But yours—"

"I knew I'd lose them, Blake," Eris murmurs, kissing my cheek and holding me tight. "I knew it before I even admitted to myself that I was queer. I invited them to know the real me, and they didn't want to. I knew that would happen and I told them anyway. You make your choices, but your parents make theirs, and you have to trust them to make the right decisions. We have to live for ourselves, Bambi." Eris leans back with a teasing grin. "Now can we stop talking about our parents before I lose this erection? You're being a good little cockwarmer, I'd hate for your hard work to go to waste."

My delighted laugh transforms into a moan when Eris thrusts into me, zis mouth trailing down to my collarbone.

"Bud?"

"Yeah, Bambi?"

"Can you help me get this off?" I ask, tugging my binder. Sticking the joint in zis mouth, Eris helps me peel it off. Ze exhales smoke around my nipple as ze bites it.

I take the joint from zim, breathing through the dull pain in my knee as I ride zim. Maybe the CBD did help, because it doesn't hurt as much as I expect. Or perhaps Eris's ministrations—sucking my chest, nails digging into my thighs, fingertips rough on my clit—is enough to distract me.

I don't know where tomorrow will leave us, but tonight, I'm right where I'm meant to be. For now—however long now lasts—I'm Eris's. I tell zim that when I come again, whisper how wonderful ze is until those star-freckled cheeks are flushed. Shout Eris's name when ze pulls another orgasm from me. I hope beyond hope that tomorrow, when we're back home and back to reality, I'm still Eris's. Because Eris is mine, even if ze can't trust that yet.

Fifteen

AFTER

THE RIDE HOME IS quiet but comfortable.

We check out of the hotel (leaving an obscene tip for housekeeping on the nightstand), and stop by my parents' house on our way out of Solberg. Eris is impressed with their homegrown strain, so I text them to ask what it actually is.

Dad hasn't changed it much since the eighties, so they don't remember. But once I open the communication floodgates, Mom fills me in with a string of replies that Eris can have some seeds, and also my dad saw a roadrunner, and also I need to send her pictures from the wedding.

We take a dozen seeds for Eris to experiment with, and I restock my stash, in exchange for a picture of us dressed up for the wedding from yesterday, and another of us with Matt and Allie. After refilling the bird feeders, I check on the chickens, giving Eris ample time to fawn over the grow setup in the basement. Part of me doesn't want to leave, and yet I'm the one rushing us back into the car to get back on the road.

Our conversations are quiet, but sparse. I get the feeling that Eris, like me, doesn't really want the drive to end, or the conversations that come after it. Taking the backroads, I take us through the Driftless Area, showing Eris the winding roads along the bluffs where the forest creates a tunnel of sun-dappled shade.

We stop for a long lunch at a cafe, instead of fast food in the car like we did on the drive out. Eris drives the second half of the trip, and I spend most of my time as the passenger with zis hand on my thigh, pointing out the birds I see.

"Can I ask a question?" I ask as we cross over the glacial moraine back to the Lake Michigan lobe, almost back to home and what comes "after".

"No."

I ask anyway. "Why did you pick ze zim as your pronouns?"

Eris groans. "Goddammit, Bambi, I was so close!"

"What?"

"Stella and I were betting if you'd get up the courage to ask again."

"Bitch, you bet on me?" I smack zis arm with a laugh.

"We've had a running bet going for almost two years, and I won every time up until now. They were sure you'd work up the courage by the time we got back, but I thought I terrified you too much the first time you asked that there was no way!"

I scoff. "I was not terrified! You said it was none of my fucking business, so I was minding my own fucking business, and now I feel like I'm allowed in your fucking business."

Eris laughs. "I love fucking with you, dude. You take everything so literally, it's hilarious. Adrienne was so pissed, she thought I'd scared you off."

I roll my eyes. "Are you gonna answer the question or not?"

"Yeah, yeah, chill out." Eris merges into the left lane to pass a semi. "I started using they them back in college, but my friends all said it was too confusing because of the 'they is plural' bullshit and never bothered. And they them didn't really fit me either." Eris pats my thigh. "No offense, but they them is too…quiet for me. I present fem, but I'm also masc, and I'm obnoxious and loud, and I love that about me. I don't want to be anything inauthentically me, and my body is part of who I am, and I don't want to change it. That's why I stay hairy and don't pitch up my voice or anything." Eris pauses, then adds, "You and Stella, you both blend in better. Not saying that you're any less you or anything, but the way you express yourself is more accepted than mine."

I nod, because that's part of the reason I find Eris so interesting. Zis unabashed, stubborn pride in zimself has always made me envious. Even though I am not naturally a loud person, I aspire to zis confidence in rocking the boat.

"Anyway, I lost the bullshit friends, and I tried out different neopronouns instead that reflect me better. Like, most people look at me and see a man in a dress and make-up."

"You're not a man in a dress," I murmur, tracing the back of zis fingers on my thigh. "You're Eris."

Eris shoots me a grin, squeezing my thigh, and my heart thumps in my chest. "I appreciate that *you* don't see me that way. But that doesn't change that most people do, and I can't control anyone's perception but my own. So if I get to fuck with their idea of what men look like, so be it. I've learned to embrace that and take pride in that, so ze zim zis fits where I'm at right now. My masculinity has been zhuzhed up into something unrecognizable that makes people uncomfortable, and I love that."

The rest of the drive continues like that, sharing all the things we want to know about each other, flirting through roasting each other, and exchanging smiles. By the time Eris pulls into the parking lot of the dispensary, where ze lives in an apartment upstairs, my cheeks ache from laughing, but my heart is in my stomach. I don't want the "now" to end, and the "after" to begin. I'm quietly terrified that Eris will withdraw, pretend this weekend never happened to protect zis heart.

But I need to find out what "after" looks like if ze doesn't.

So after I help Eris get zis bags out of the back, I pull zim close into a hug before ze can withdraw and hide inside. "Thank you for everything, Eris."

"You, too, Blake." Patting my back, Eris tries to step away. But I cling tight, counting to five under my breath. "What are you doing?" ze asks.

"Waiting until we've been home for longer than five seconds before asking you out."

To my delight, Eris cackles. "Goddammit, you take everything so literally."

"Yeah, aspiring lawyer, remember?" I tease.

Eris huffs and pulls me tight against zim. The tote bags bang against my knees as ze rises on zis tiptoes to kiss me, lips crushing against mine. "It's so fucking annoying, Bambi."

"You like it." I grin and kiss zim back.

"Ugh, just lock your damn car." Handing me the bags, Eris waits until my car beeps to pick me up and carry me into zis building. My laugh comes out as a squeal as I wrap my legs around zis waist and cling to zim harder than ever.

Eris can pretend to be annoyed all ze wants, but I see how the star field scattered across zis cheeks flushes. The way those doe eyes widen when I kiss zis cheek. The smirk highlighted by those snakebite scars before ze presses zis lips against mine. I see through Eris, just like ze sees through me.

Ze was just as scared as me, scared I'd forget everything we've shared this weekend and revert to the lost recluse I've been for the past two years.

But I'm done shaping my life around everyone else. No more people-pleasing, no more letting anyone make my decisions, even out of spite. I have to live my life for me, all-encompassing and unshrinkable and unapologetic.

More than anything, I want to prove to Eris that I meant every word last night: I'm not going anywhere, whatever our future holds. I want to break free of the cluttered gloom of my life, for Eris to show me the friendship and laughter, warmth and love I've been missing out on. I want to leave behind the spiteful shell I've planted myself in, step into the sun, and see what blooms from these petty roots.

Epilogue

ERIS

BLAKE RYAN IS SUCH a fucking nerd.

They had all week to clean their apartment—three hundred square feet of clutter. The whole month really, ever since they confirmed that their parents, Matt, and Allie were all coming down for a visit. Blake took the bar last week, and they start work at their new job on Monday; they finally invited their loved ones to visit when they'd have a few days to decompress and relax, but before they get busy with work.

Basically, my grumpy, messy, stressed out Bambi has had *so* much time to tidy up.

And yet, as I'm getting ready to go out to eat in the bathroom, Blake starts panic-cleaning their apartment—a mere hour before we're supposed to leave—just in case everyone else asks to come visit after dinner. Even though we're meeting everyone at some pizza place in the Loop, a half hour away by train, and they just got into town today.

"Bro, even if they ask to come, you can say no. You know that, right?" I shove my makeup bag and work clothes into my tote bag on the couch. My blue maxi dress is a little wrinkled after spending all day crumpled up next to my water bottle and keys, but I'll still probably look more presentable than Blake. This dress is cute as fuck on me too, even with the wrinkles. "You just took the bar a week ago. That's the perfect excuse to get out of giving them the grand tour."

Frantically washing dishes in stained joggers and a T-shirt with a hole where they ripped the tag out of it, Blake glares at me over their shoulder. "It's the principle. I should be able to have my parents visit me without feeling an overwhelming sense of shame."

It takes everything in me not to laugh at their stress; Blake seems to thrive in it. For someone so structured and driven on the surface, they are a complete slob who procrastinates whenever they can get away with it. Instead of teasing them for their dramatics, I simply kiss their shoulder and smack their ass on my way to the overflowing trash bin to make myself useful.

"Wait!" Blake says, their green eyes wide and frantic. "I don't have all the garbage in there yet."

I glance down at the heap of trash that's already going to be a bitch to tie shut. "There's no room for more."

"But I can't take the garbage out yet. Not until it's all bagged up."

I press my lips together and busy myself with tying up the bag anyway, but Blake catches my shoulders shaking.

"Stop laughing at me!" Blake huffs. But when I glance up, they're fighting a smile.

"I'm not laughing at *you*," I insist, pulling the bag out of the bin. "I am laughing at all these damn rules you follow that don't make a lick of sense."

"It makes perfect sense!" Blake flicks water at me. "I can do it all in one trip!"

"Okay, but this shit is overflowing, so I'm gonna take it out now. And then you can take it out again when you get the rest of it together." I slide my feet into my platform shoes by the door. From the sink, Blake glares at me. I stare back at them, a little too long. Pink creeps into their pale face, and they straighten their back ever so slightly. Those green eyes that caught my attention two years ago widen, and my chest warms with just how fucking precious this nerd is. "We have an hour before we have to leave. If you're good and get everything all cleaned up, and if we have time, I'll make you come before we leave."

"Eris!" Blake's face flushes deeper. "Stop distracting me!"

That wasn't a no. I smirk as I haul the trash into the hallway. "Dishes, Bambi!"

By the time I'm back from the alley behind Blake's building, the dishes are in a haphazard pile to dry, and Blake is scrubbing the countertop with all their might. Their ass and thighs jiggle in their joggers with the force of their elbow grease, and I melt, imagining kneeling behind them with my face buried between those perfect, round cheeks. For a nerd who spends most of their days curled up over their laptop like a shrimp, Blake Ryan has the best ass.

"You said *everything* had to be clean first," Blake reminds me when I tease the waistline of their joggers.

"Did I?" I wrap my arms around them, kissing their shoulder. "I lied. I just meant the dishes." Blake laughs, then goes quiet in my arms, fussing with a crusty spot on the counter. Very unlike their usual, eager, freaky self. I frown. Normally, they're begging for me to touch them within seconds at the mere suggestion of sex. "What's wrong?"

"Can we..." Blake sighs, and the sound makes dread pool in the pit in my stomach. "Can we raincheck the orgasm until after dinner?"

Is that all? Relived, I nod into their neck. "Of course," I squeeze them tight once more, then give them some space, backing away to lean against the counter next to them. Blake pouts, but doesn't look at me. I hate how my first thought is always that they're about to break up with me. It's only been a month, but every day has been a dream, and Blake already wants me to meet their parents. Everything should be happy. I hate this sense of constant dread hanging over me; it's bad enough that I'm considering going to therapy again. "Everything okay?"

"I'm nervous," Blake admits, tossing the sponge in the sink to wash their hands.

"*You're* nervous?" I tease, fussing with a wrinkle in my skirt. "I'm about to meet your parents. I'm not exactly who you'd bring home to convince them you're doing okay, remember?" With a whine, Blake cringes, and I regret bringing that up. "Sorry, that was supposed to be a lighthearted joke."

Blake groans as they dry their hands on the towel. "I was such a dick to you. I'm sorry. I should never have said that."

"Bambi, I thought it was funny. Then and now. You're so fucking rude sometimes, it's hilarious. Besides, it's not untrue." I catch their hands before they find some other mess to tidy up, rubbing circles into their palms. I don't know what it says about me that I'm more confident that Blake actually likes me when they insult me, but I never want them to stop. "It's going to be okay. Matt and Allie will be there, right? And your parents seem chill, from everything you've told me. Everything will be okay."

"I'm not nervous about them meeting you, Eris," Blake mutters. They give another one of those sighs that hit me right in the insecurity, but they lean their head against mine. The tension leaks out of them with each press of my thumbs into their palms. A twinge of pain makes my right wrist ache, but I keep massaging their hand until Blake is limp and relaxed against me. "I just haven't told them that I'm staying in Chicago now that I've graduated, or about my job that fucking starts on Monday! I haven't told them I'm starting T. I haven't told them we've only been dating one month, instead of four." Forehead still pressed to my temple, they shake their head, whispering, "I'm nervous that I'll disappoint them. I've been keeping so much from them."

"You think they'll be disappointed? In *you*? Bambi, you graduated from law school, passed the bar—" I press my lips to Blake's when they start to interrupt me; I already know they won't get their results for months. We've had this conversation six times, but I don't need the official results to know they passed. I kiss away the argument that they don't need to start until Blake once again relaxes against me, wrapping their arms around my shoulders. "And you got hired by your dream law firm months before you graduated. You really think that they'll be disappointed that you're such an uptight, nerdy ass overachiever?

Because a month ago, you bagged a total baddie. So even your romance and social life isn't nearly as pathetic as it was."

"Shut up," Blake mutters, but they're smiling.

"They love you, and they want you to be happy. Right? And you hope that this job will make you happy?" Blake nods, closing their eyes as I rub their back. "And starting T?" Another nod from them. I swallow. The pit of my stomach aches again, but I force myself to ask, "Staying here? Will that make you happy?"

Eyes snapping open, Blake glares at me. It's so fucking sweet, those big green eyes narrowed in annoyance. Their long nose, all scrunched up, brushes mine. I adore that I'm the one who gets to see their grumpy face so often, because they are always so careful about concealing what a snarky ass bitch they are from everyone. Except me. I get to see every single version of Blake they think they need to hide. Each glare is an honor to witness. Each weird vocal stim is a treasure I cherish. With no question or hesitation, I get to see the lazy slob and anxious wreck they don't want their parents, friends, or strangers to see.

"What?" I finally ask after staring into Blake's narrowed eyes for longer than they probably want, but it's taking everything not to kiss them right now.

"I'm not dignifying that with a response."

"I dunno, Bambi, you're trying to murder me with your eyes right now. It might be a no—"

This time, Blake shuts *me* up with a kiss. It's mean and demanding, their lips hard against mine. Like I kissed the fight out of them earlier, Blake's kiss is full of reassurance, and the hollow of insecurity eases.

"Will you help me?" Blake asks quietly when they pull away.

"With what?" I ask, wishing I could feel as peaceful as this all the time. "You want *me* to tell them you start your new job on Monday?"

"No, just..." Blake sighs, banging their forehead against mine again. "Mom won't try to, but she just...I don't want them to mow down my flowers."

This bitch and their nature metaphors. I smile, pressing a kiss to their cheek. "Let them see how beautifully you're blooming, then."

Blake wrinkles their nose. "That's corny, Bud."

"You started it." My hands slide under their shirt, along the warm, smooth skin of their back. "I'll be right there, okay? I will probably be saying the wrong thing and making a horrible first impression, but I can find a spot in the conversation for you to bring it up, and I'll be right there to back you up the whole time. Is that what you need?" Blake nods. "Okay. And if you're good..." I trail off suggestively, pulling Blake a little closer to me.

"Define good," Blake smirks.

"Well, first, you wanted to clean this place, and you still have trash everywhere." I tighten my grip around their waist before they can start panic-cleaning again. "And you have four things you want to tell them. That's five orgasms to earn, Bambi." I glance down at their ratty T-shirt and stained joggers. "Six if you get dressed into something a little more presentable? I mean, you do you, but we did make reservations for this place weeks ago."

"I was gonna change after I finished cleaning!" Blake laughs, pushing me away. "You're such a dick!"

I beam. "You like it."

"Whatever." Blake throws an empty soda can at me.

"Hey, watch the dress! This is Dream's!" I toss the can into the cardboard box acting as a recycling bin, then smooth down the skirt of the pretty blue cotton dress I've been indefinitely borrowing from Dream for years. Everything looks good on her, and this is one of the few casual dresses I've found that hangs nicely on me. "Fucking brat."

"You like it." Blake kisses my cheek before they put a fresh bag in the trash can. Tempting as it is to keep flirting, to keep distracting them, we actually do have to leave soon. It's embarrassing how nervous I am for this. I've spent my whole life trying to become this nonchalant jackass who doesn't give a fuck. But I do give a fuck. A lot of fucks. After an adulthood filled with cynicism and hardship, the past year has been good. Great, even. And the past month, unbelievably, indescribably...wonderful. With Blake, with our friends, with my life, I'm really happy.

I don't trust it to last, but I want it to. Blake loves their parents, and I refuse to let meeting the Ryans become an opportunity to sabotage my happiness. I can be a polite, charming jackass for one weekend. Showing up to dinner disheveled and reeking of sex, tempting as it is, would not make a great first impression.

I WAS REALLY HOPING that Matt and Allie would show up at the same time as the Ryans, to help buffer the awkwardness. Because from what Blake's told me, their parents are just as awkward as they are.

However, when Blake and I walk in (Blake now dressed in a boxy tank top and their "nice" joggers), Linda and Michael are sitting alone at the restaurant. My partner's cinnamon roll ex and hilarious bestie are nowhere to be seen in the corner booth. The pizza parlor is loud and dark and crowded, and I have to drop Blake's hand to follow them through the walkways between the tables. I press my hands against my thighs through my dress, trying not to clench the fabric; I'd been more confident before, but without Blake's hand in mine, nerves get the better of me. I'm not used to trying to be polite or charming; being a genderfuck weirdo is a comfortable armor against the inevitable rejection.

As she gets up to hug Blake, Linda surprises me with how tall she is, with frizzy red hair piled high on her head in a haphazard bun. For some reason, I'd assumed Blake got their height from their dad, but no. Linda is a couple inches taller than me, even with my platforms. "Blakey-poo! Finally! My baby child!"

"Hi Mom," Blake mutters into their mom's shoulder when she pulls them into a tight hug.

"And you must be Eris!" Linda turns to me next, and my nerves seize in my chest. She presses her lips together in a smile, looking at me up and down with a nod. "Your hair is really shiny, though you're shorter than I thought you'd be. The tattoos are rad, and your dress is cute!" She looks at her own chambray dress. "We almost match!"

Dream's floral blue sundress looks nothing like Linda's, but I just say, "Yeah, blue!" because I don't know what else to say to that. I doubt Linda would appreciate my teasing as much as Blake does, and I'm trying to make a good impression here.

With no other warning than a "Hug!" as it happens, my face is squeezed into Linda's shoulder. I tentatively pat her on the back, unsure of how I missed the signs she was going for it. Like Blake at their most unfiltered, Linda seems to talk fast, state her observations out loud, and doesn't consider how her words might land. It won't give me much to work with to keep a conversation going, but I suspect that won't be an issue with Linda like it can be with Blake.

It took months of drag brunches to figure out Blake's tells, to adapt my own abrasive personality to draw them out of their shell. But Blake was a fascinating puzzle to solve, a subtle language I had to learn before I could get closer to the interesting person behind the mask. Linda is Blake at their most carefree. No mask at all.

"This is my husband, Michael." Linda gestures to the quiet man half hidden behind her. He's tall, too, wearing a sun hat and utility vest over a green polo. Looking like a park ranger, even though it's six in the evening in downtown Chicago.

"Pleasure to meet you, sir," I nod, keeping an eye out for any sign of a handshake. Or another hug. Blake said he doesn't have the best mobility in his right hand, so on the rare occasions he initiates a handshake, I should use my left. But Michael simply nods at me, gestures to his ears, and mouths something I can't hear, but what looks to roughly mean, *It's nice to meet you too, but it's very loud in here.*

"He's got earplugs in," Linda explains. "He gets tired when there are too many things to listen to, and it was such a long drive today." She waves us into the circular booth. "Eris, come sit by me, so I can ask you everything!"

Face blank, Blake gives me a shrug, so I scoot to the back of the round booth, while Linda slides in before her husband on the other side. If this is how their parents communicate, I can see why Blake has a hard time asserting themself.

Blake winces as they push themself around the table to be next to me. "Matt and Allie not here yet?" they ask their mom as they fight to get their knee around the table leg. I offer them a hand to pull them the rest of the way around the booth. Blake, independent as always, swats it away. They let me help relieve their pain, and I'm allowed to harass them about their PT, but they're stubborn about doing everything for themself.

"They took a nap after the drive, and they were just getting up when it was time to leave. They should be along any moment." Linda waves a hand. "So, Eris, what do you do?"

"Mom, I already told you—"

"I know, I know, but I want to hear it from Eris."

I am immediately irritated for Blake, who clams up, no grumpy face in sight. When I feel their huff of annoyance against my side, not loud enough to hear, it takes extra effort not to answer with my usual surly "drug dealer." My default response always gives me a good read on someone based on how they react. But from the grow room setup in their basement, Linda wouldn't even blink. "I am the retail manager at a dispensary."

"And ze's a contractor for the state in breeding experimental medical strains," Blake adds. I nod, still weirded out that I'm technically a government contractor *and* a manager. Even though my days are spent helping people get high and making cannabis plants fuck, this is the least punk job I've had since I've been on my own. I have fucking health insurance. And PTO.

"As a person of color in the cannabis industry," Linda starts, and I cringe internally. Oh god, where is she going with this? Linda purses her lips, green eyes narrowing. "What are your thoughts on gentrification of a previously criminalized industry?"

I take Blake's hand under the table to keep myself from laughing, because Linda's expression is exactly like Blake's surly face. Luckily, Blake laces their fingers through mine, giving me a tight squeeze, as if I'm reaching for their support instead of a reminder to not laugh at their mother. "It's bad?"

Instead of the amusement I was hoping for, Linda's eyebrows do most of the talking, a quick raise demanding more. Next to her, Michael pulls a crossword book out of his vest and gets to work. Blake's face is still eerily impassive, to a degree I haven't seen since I first met them. Tough crowd.

"And I think the for-profit prison industry should be abolished, and the whole joke of a criminal justice system reformed completely?" I add with a shrug, curious how Linda will take that. I have no idea what Linda is hoping I'll say; this is not the line of questioning I'd expect from meeting a partner's parents. But knowing Blake, I should have guessed.

Linda purses her lips, frown lines deepening. But if she's anything like Blake, that might be a good facial expression?

Thankfully, the hot himbo puppy dog and the secretly bitchy Barbie doll show up before Linda can ask me to elaborate, because I don't really want to talk about prison abolition before we've even ordered drinks. I'd been wondering how we would manage the inevitable hugs when Blake was already struggling getting into the booth, but Matt solves that problem by draping himself over Blake to plant a wet kiss on my cheek. "Eris! You look gorgeous as ever! Love that color on you! How are you? Any new tattoos? I love your makeup!"

My face burns, because good lord, how did Blake ever leave this man behind? He smells fabulously masculine, his shoulders are built like a fucking longhorn steer, and he's such a damn flirt, with that crooked grin and freckled nose. His face is way too close to be platonic as he rubs my cheek with his thumb.

"Get off of me!" Blake grumbles, trapped beneath Matt's ribcage next to me.

Matt simply laughs and tucks Blake into a headlock, smooching the crown of their head in greeting. He clambers back out of the booth to let Allie sit next to Blake, who showers them in warm affection, too.

If Matt reminds me of a golden retriever, Allie reminds me of a barn cat: cute and sweet from a distance, but with sharp claws and teeth at the ready. Her blonde hair is pulled back into a high pony, ample chest and curves on display in a light blue tank top. She greets me with a knowing smirk over Blake's shoulder as she hugs them.

Instead of a hello, I stick my tongue out at her. Just one look, and that weird, instant friendship we jumped feetfirst into over a bottle of champagne at the wedding is back. It feels like we've spent every day together for years, instead of a few hours together one day a month ago.

Blake never stood a fucking chance. I barely know these two and—not that I'm particularly inclined to polyamory or open relationships—if Blake ever wanted to have a foursome with their ex and their former crush, I would be down. They're both good people, and incredibly attractive.

With the new additions to the group, the feeling of being so incredibly trapped builds as the conversation carries on around us. I fight to relax as my fists clench my skirt. On one side, Matt is rapid-firing questions to everyone at the table, and tossing compliments my way like grenades. On the other, Linda is sharing her opinion about any subject Matt brings up, including the things he's complimenting me on. It's almost worse that she agrees with him, because I never know how to take compliments. Allie keeps smirking as if she knows how uncomfortable I am, and Michael is at the end of the table, ignoring us all in favor of his crossword.

Through it all, Blake is still uncannily blank. Their eyes blink sometimes, and their jaw is tight, but other than that, there is no sign of my Bambi. If we were at brunch, this is when I'd say something out of pocket, just to draw them out of their shell and annoy them. But I don't know what their mom would think of it. Admittedly, our rapport does not look healthy on the surface. Kelsey and Dream think it's weird how mean Blake and I are to each other, but Stella and Adrienne get that it's basically foreplay for us.

Instead, I make myself let go of the fabric balled up in my fist to take their hand again, pressing my thumb into their palm. "Uh...should we order?" I ask, gesturing to the sign on the table.

Blake nods solemnly, and scans the QR code. "Mom, you and Dad want a bottle of white?"

"Oh, is this one of those code places?" Linda scoffs. "I knew we were going downhill as a society when people stopped taking cash, but now they can't even take our orders?"

"I like being able to scroll the menu," Blake shrugs. "I'm sure if you want a server, we could ask for one."

Linda waves a hand. "Well, no, I don't want to be a bother. I just think the farther we get from a bartering economy, the unhappier we will be."

"It is really weird to tip the drag queens with Venmo instead of bills," I nod in agreement. "But that's on me for never carrying cash anymore."

Blake hisses quietly next to me, just a sharp intake of breath. My stomach sinks. How did I fuck up with *that* topic? I thought their parents would be fine with drag, considering their child is trans.

"Drag queens?" Linda's frown is back. "Now there's an interesting question! Eris, as a non-binary person, what are your thoughts on—"

"You're going to drag brunch tomorrow morning, right?" Matt blurts out, his eyes wide as he exchanges a glance with Blake. "Could we come with you? Allie and I?" He smiles sympathetically at Linda. "I don't know if it'd be your speed."

Linda laughs mockingly. "Please, I've been to more drag shows than years you've been alive, young man! Back in the day, I was quite the hag."

"Mom!" Blake's face is beet red; they look like they're about to slide under the table in embarrassment. "You're not allowed to say that!"

I lose my composure, cracking up despite my best efforts to behave. All of this is so ridiculous. Why the fuck was I expecting their parents to be so proper and polite?

"What?" Linda waves a hand. "See? Eris thinks it's funny!"

I just laugh harder when Blake glares at me.

"Eris has a really twisted sense of humor, Linda," Allie explains. "I wouldn't rely on zim finding something funny as a good metric."

"Bitch!" I mouth at her behind my hand, my shoulders still shaking.

Smug, Allie smirks back at me, a silent, *"Takes one to know one."*

"So, yeah, we can come to brunch with you in the morning?" Matt prompts.

"I can ask if we can add to the reservation," I say, since Blake is in shrimp-mode next to me in the booth, face buried in their phone under the guise of ordering food for everyone. I lean towards Linda, hoping she'll say no, but asking anyway, to be polite. "Do you want to come?"

"I assume it'll be loud?" Linda asks, glancing at Michael next to her.

I nod. "Very. And it's outside, so it'll be hot, too."

Waving her hand again in that vague dismissal, Linda shakes her head. "We'll just meet you for a late lunch then!"

I send a quick text to Dream, who immediately responds that she will bribe the host tomorrow as much as it takes to make room for "Blake's fool of an ex and the man-stealing best friend," because she and Kelsey have been dying of curiosity to meet them.

"So...anything you're looking forward to seeing while you're here?" I ask Linda, hoping that simple question doesn't turn into a philosophical debate. The polite question feels flat and fake. From the weird looks Matt and Allie are giving me, it sounded that way too.

The Ryans, Blake included, don't seem to have noticed. "Anything my baby wants us to see!" Linda beams proudly at Blake, who groans and sinks deeper into the booth. Sometimes I forget Blake is younger than me; it's validating that they have their immature moments too. "But Michael wanted to go to the natural history museum, so we might do that while you're having brunch."

"We could meet you there after?" It feels so weird, being the nice one at the table, instead of the surly jackass judging everyone from the sidelines with a snarky comment from time to time. I don't like it. But Blake is still looking weird and blank, and everyone else here is technically their guest. This is what partners do, right? Act like a host, or whatever? "We could walk along the lakefront, and there's a tapas place with a patio overlooking the pier we could go to for lunch."

"That sounds perfect!" Allie chimes in.

"Perfect, the plan is settled!" Linda nods with a bright hum. "So, Eris, how much career stability and growth potential do you see in the cannabis industry, given that it's such a young and heavily regulated industry?"

A pang of annoyance burns inside me, and I do my best to swallow it. Linda is definitely a professor, answering every question while she's asking it.

"Linda, that's a leading question!" Allie teases. She's so good at correcting people, while keeping up that sweet facade. Matt looks on, hanging on his wife's every word with a proud, affectionate smile, and zero thoughts inside that pretty head. "Maybe a better question to ask would be, 'Where do you see your career going?'"

"That's not what I asked, though, is it?" Linda rolls her eyes. "That's a boring job interview question. I don't want a boring job interview answer. I want Eris's insider expertise on where he-" Linda pauses as she corrects herself on the pronoun, "*ze* sees the industry going, given the risk and industry fragility."

"You want my honest answer?" I challenge. If Linda doesn't want a job interview answer, I'll give her the real one. The nonchalant jackass answer, instead of the charming response I probably should give.

Blake puts their phone down next to me with a quiet sigh. I pat their thigh under the table, hoping it's reassuring, but not really caring. Blake might wear a mask around their parents, but I don't want to. While I could, it's uncomfortable. I can be less abrasive without faking politeness. I am with everyone else who has made it past the repulsive exterior, why not Blake's parents? Blake looks over at me expectantly, but they show no hint of disapproval or encouragement behind their mask. My only clue that they won't be upset is the hand that softly touches my "And I say fuck it!" tattoo on my forearm.

With a frown, Linda nods for me to continue.

"I don't fucking know where any of this is going. I don't know how I ended up in this job in the first place. I stumble through life, figuring shit out as I go." I set my jaw, daring Linda's frown to argue with me. "This is a good job, don't get me wrong, and I hope I can keep it, but if I can't? I'll stumble somewhere else. But I always land on my feet."

It's the wrong answer for meeting the parents. I'm supposed to say I have a five-year plan and a solid job record and bullshit. But it wouldn't be true. I was getting by okay as a tattoo artist, and I'm getting by easier now as a cannabis scientist and retail manager of the dispensary. My parents always had so many plans for me that I never had a say in, and I don't want to limit myself the way they expected me to.

Already, this job has way too much responsibility, too much *respectability*, for my taste. But I'm thirty-two, with arthritis that keeps me from the art that used to nourish me. I can't even sketch for more than an hour at a time anymore without needing three days of extra-strength pain meds. At this point, I can stomach a bit of respectability if it means being comfortable.

To my surprise, Linda nods approvingly, despite the frown. "I like that attitude! Land on your feet! That's on period!"

"No," Blake immediately says. "Please don't say that, Mom."

I bite back my laugh, because there'd be some exasperation mixed in that might hurt Blake's feelings if they're already stressed. Blake has barely said a word this whole time, other than telling their mom what not to say. While Linda seems to be prone to saying the wrong thing, I think I like her, overall. My own mother would never have accepted me working in any risky industry, let alone not showing an ounce of ambition in my work. Linda not only accepts it, she seems to support it.

"My students say it all the time!" Linda protests.

"Doesn't make it okay," Blake sighs.

"Remember that link I sent you, Linda?" Matt asks. "The one about Gen Z slang?"

"Oh, is that one of those appropriation phrases?" Linda asks. "I had no idea! I thought it was just what the kids were saying." She pats my arm with another hum; so many of Blake's weird mouth sounds and vocal stims make so much sense after meeting their mom. "So what's the plan for September?"

"What's in September?" I ask.

"When Blake's lease is up?" Linda prompts. "Are you two going to do long-distance when they move back, or something?" She trails off.

Oh wow, Blake really did not even hint to their mom they were staying. Stomach sinking, I glance at Blake, who is staring at the table like they're actively wishing for a hole in the floor to open up and swallow them. I don't know what I expected, given what fucking doormat Blake can be. Still, the disappointment stings as it leaks into the cracks formed by insecurity. Shouldn't they be excited about this? About their future here? With me?

However, Blake asked for my help to push the conversation, and this is the chance they wanted to clear the air. I can set my hurt aside and freak out for later when I'm alone. "Uh...I think Blake might be the one to answer that question," I mutter, prompting Blake with a squeeze of their thigh under my hand.

"Blake?" Linda asks, cocking her head. "Anything to share?"

Eyes wide, Matt looks like he's about to interrupt again, change the subject. I shake my head, jaw tight. This is something Blake wants to tell their parents today. This is their opportunity. So why aren't they saying anything? I swallow hard, mouth dry. Blake just sits there, expressionless.

Allie looks from Blake to me, giving me an encouraging smile. *"Still waters, "*she mouths, a reminder of the conversation we had in the bridal suite last month. We were hiding together so she could vent about everything weighing on her, and ask me everything about my relationship with Blake. Blake and I were supposed to be faking a history that didn't exist, but I never bothered to keep up the pretense with Allie. Somehow, I could tell she'd know I was lying, so I just told her everything. Including many things I hadn't told Blake yet.

She wasn't surprised, because Blake is a terrible liar, and I obviously had feelings for them (obvious to everyone but Blake, anyway).They're someone who hides everything, internalizes it, and only a privileged few get to witness the real Blake. Allie warned me then, that if I was going to stick around, I should know how special they were, and treat them accordingly, be someone they could trust to open up around.

Until a month ago, Blake hadn't had someone like that since they moved to Chicago. Blake lost that trust in their parents when they pushed them to fit in, instead of be themself in high school. They lost that trust in Matt when he broke up with them, and in Allie when she asked if Blake would be mad if something happened between her and Matt. Blake never blamed any of them, never held any anger or bitterness against them, because Blake is understanding and loyal. And, according to Allie, because they never know what the fuck they're feeling until the pain has healed.

Everything Allie told me that afternoon was true. Blake is so bright, so full of life, but only when it's just us. They're getting more open around our friends in private, but not to the degree of when we're alone together. *"Still waters run deep with Blake,"* Allie had said. The calmer they are, the more they're freaking out. When they're overwhelmed, they shut down.

I haven't seen that quiet, reclusive version of Blake since their argument with Jessica at the rehearsal dinner. Since the polite walls between us broke completely, and we saw each other for who we were, what we wanted. We've seen each other's meltdowns and freak outs, and we've worked through them together.

The blank person next to me, with the polite mask as they mull over an answer is not okay. Blake needs more than me at their side—they need to trust I have their back. And I have to trust they have mine, because I'm freaking out too, panicking that they're taking so long to answer this simple question, with a prepared answer they were practicing on the train ride over. I'm terrified they're taking so long because they're working up the courage to say they're moving back, that they might choose to leave me.

I have to trust they won't.

I pull Blake's hand from where it's clenched on top of their knees, working my thumb under their fingers to press against their palm.

Fist slowly unclenching in my hands, Blake takes a deep breath, then another. Looking at the table, they blurt out, "I haven't gotten to explore the city yet. And I have an appointment with a gender therapist who can help me start HRT. And with work— Oh, I start my new job on Monday! I guess, I just..." Blake trails off when they look up at their mom for her approval, but Linda simply nods for them to finish. "I want to stay. I'm staying. I'll be happier staying." Their eyes flick to me, and the slightest blush blooms on their cheeks as they lace their fingers with mine. "Oh, and Eris and I have only been together for a month, since the wedding. I lied to Matt and Allie about seeing someone here, and Eris helped me cover my ass by pretending to be my partner, and we just decided to keep being partners for real." They smile at me. It's quiet, just a slight curve of their petal pink lips, but a real smile all the same. "Did I get them all? My orgasms?"

A laugh escapes me, and I'm too relieved to see a hint of the real Blake to care that their mother just heard that. "Yeah, Bambi, you got them all. We'll settle up later, though. In private."

"Fuck," Blake bangs their head on my shoulder. "I said all of that the wrong way."

"It was perfect," I squeeze their hand. "You're perfect, Bambi."

"Well!" Linda sighs loudly, politely ignoring any references to orgasms. "So much to take in all at once, but it sounds like you've got everything under control, and you've put a lot of thought into this!" She smiles at the server, who finally brings us the bottles of wine Blake ordered. "Excuse me, dear? Can you also bring a bottle of champagne? We have so much to celebrate!"

"Tell us all about your new job!" Allie prompts Blake, even though she's fully aware of what Blake's job is.

"I'll be a junior associate at an environmental law firm," Blake says, directing it to their mom. "They specialize in environmental policy."

"Oh, Blakey-poo!" Linda beams. She pats Michael's arm, who takes an earplug out. "Blake got a job here in Chicago. They'll be working at an environmental law firm, starting Monday!"

"Oh! That's great! I was wondering what the plan was." Michael smiles, nodding approvingly. His smile is just like Blake's, a little awkward and unsure, but so bright and genuine. "I'm proud of you, kiddo!"

Blake relaxes, leaning against my arm. "Thanks, Dad."

A weird pressure forms in my chest as I watch this awkward ass family connect in their own awkward ass way. Blake's parents remind me of my own, a bit, except my parents are much cooler. Heartless assholes, like I try so hard to emulate, but effortlessly confident and social. My mother was also exacting and demanding, but where Mom was inflexible in her expectations, Linda seems to simply want the best for her family. Dad was just as distant as Michael, but I don't think I ever heard him say he was proud of me. If he did, it never came so easily as Michael's approval just now.

It's hard to know what Linda and Michael might think of me, with everything that comes with being the alt genderfuck baddie that I am, but I hope they like me. I'm sure Michael is more engaging when he's not tired and overstimulated. And when we're more comfortable with each other, Linda and I will have many interesting debates ahead of us. She's the only other person at this table who doesn't seem to break out in hives at the thought of conflict, anyway.

The server returns with a bottle of champagne and a tray of glasses. Matt passes the glasses around the table to us as he fills them. "What are we toasting to?" he asks.

"To your wedding, for one!" Linda waves her glass between Matt and Allie. "To my beloved child graduating from law school, and passing the bar—"

"I don't get my results until October," Blake starts, but I cut them off with a groan.

"Bambi, you literally said it was easier than you were expecting," I huff.

"That doesn't mean I passed," Blake mutters. "I don't want to get my hopes up."

"In that case, we're toasting that my beloved child thought the bar was easy!" Linda exchanges an exasperated look with me. "To new relationships! And to Eris for joining our family!"

Surprised, I can only blink, eyes burning. *Joining their family?* They just met me.

It's Blake's turn to squeeze my hand, as if sensing the panic seizing my chest. Forget feeling trapped, everything in me is screaming to run, to crawl under the booth and leave now, so I never have to feel the disappointment when it turns out they were just being polite. But the fingers laced with mine are telling me to stay, that I can belong here in this weird family, if I want to.

Linda thankfully doesn't notice my attachment issues exploding in my head. She turns to her husband. "Michael, anything you want to toast to?"

Michael thinks for a second. "Uh...Sue."

"Sue?" Linda frowns.

"That's the dinosaur at the museum you're going to tomorrow," Blake explains.

Linda simply nods. "Oh, okay! To Sue, then!" She raises her glass.

"To Sue," we say, as we all *clink* glasses. Weirdest fucking toast ever, honoring a fossil when there's so much else to celebrate. However, this is Blake's party, and somehow a toast to a dinosaur fits them perfectly.

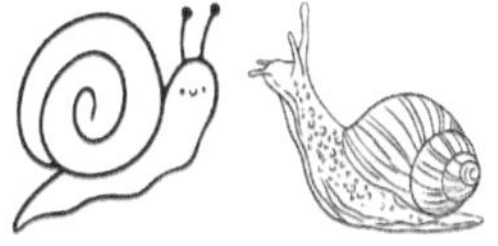

"Your dad eats deep dish with a knife and fork. He went through six moist towelettes, which he brought from home, because he didn't like when the food touched his mouth." I toss my keys on the entry table as I shut my front door behind Blake. "And he brought his crossword puzzle to dinner. You really don't see this?"

Considering how worked up they got about cleaning their place, Blake asked to stay at mine after dinner. They never need an excuse to stay, but Blake always comes up with one, whether it's to use my washing machine, or because my couch is easier on their back when they're up late studying. Tonight, it's because my place is closer to the Loop, so it'll be easier to collect Matt and Allie on our way to Boystown in the morning.

Personally, I think it's because my apartment actually feels like a home, and not just an undecorated, cluttered closet where Blake sleeps, eats, and studies.

"Yeah, but that doesn't mean he's autistic." Blake spreads the waterproof blanket down before they flop on the couch. "With his CP, eating is easier when he takes small bites. The cheese was really sticky. And he just really likes word puzzles."

"He gets tired when the music is too loud." Not bothering to turn on the light (Blake hates overhead lighting, and the glow from the city through the window is enough to see by), I climb on top of them, wrapping my arms under their back. I love how Blake assumes we're going to fuck immediately, on the couch, the second we're home. Normally, we probably would, but the person I'm holding still isn't my Bambi. Not entirely. The mask is still on, and it's hard for me to get a read on them when they're hiding from me like they do everyone else. Blake's hand traces along my neck, making me shudder at their featherlight touch. "Your mom also seems more than a little neurodivergent. Might run in the family?"

"For the last time, I'm not autistic," Blake laughs.

"Please, Stella peer-reviewed you within minutes the first time we met." I tease as I kiss the bare bit of skin along their neck, where their T-shirt is tugged down. "But fine, when you're ready to consider it, I'll try not to say I told you so."

After helping Stella get their diagnosis, and being Dream's official reminder person to help refill her ADHD meds (a role Adrienne has yet to steal from me), I've been confident that Blake is not neurotypical pretty much since the day we met. After dinner with their parents, any doubts I had are gone. But there's no point in pushing; if Blake never wants to acknowledge that there is a chance, I will just quietly support them however they want to be supported.

I breathe in the clean scent of Blake's skin, all of the stress and the anxiety draining out of me as they settle underneath me. I didn't realize how much tension I was carrying until now, in the comfortable familiarity of home, of snuggling with Blake on the couch.

"Was I good tonight, Bud?" Blake asks, their smirk grazing my ear.

Tempting as it is to play along, because I know where that bratty tone will lead us, this is the first sign of the real Blake I've seen in hours. Even after opening up about everything they've been hiding, Blake's mask never quite disappeared. I'm sure they want the stress relief, but I want to check in first. "You tell me," I murmur.

Blake huffs. "That was neither praise nor degradation. I want my orgasms. Six of them."

I laugh. "You'll get them, I promise, you little freak. But first, seriously, Bambi, how did tonight go for you? Did you have a good time? Are you relieved now that you shared all your secrets?"

"Oh, we're actually talking?" Blake whines. "Fine. I guess I had a good time? It was nice to see everyone."

"But you were stressed as fuck."

"Was I?" Blake asks. "Oh, I guess, yeah, but I'm always kinda stressed. And it wasn't that bad, I suppose. I got everything out that I wanted to say. I didn't say it as eloquently as I wanted, but I dunno. It was fine."

"You were great, Bambi." I hold them tighter.

But Blake isn't done; I've unlocked their ramble mode. "I just feel silly, for stressing so much about it. Like, of course they were supportive of everything. I knew they would be! So why did I convince myself for months that this would be a bigger deal than it is?"

"I mean, your mom is hella intimidating." I chuckle into their neck. "But mostly I think you freaked yourself out because you're an anxious ass bitch."

"Shut up, asshole." Blake play-bites my ear. "You're like a million times more intimidating than she is."

I shake my head; Blake is the intimidating one. Stunning, intelligent, and completely unreadable—most of the time. More often than not, when I tease them for being a nerd, it's to remind myself that they're just as sensitive as I am, because no one would ever know it until they got to know Blake.

"Did I-" I clear my throat; I was about to ask if I embarrassed them, but I don't want to know the answer to that. "Did I make a half-decent impression on your parents?"

"Eris," Blake murmurs into my hair. "Do you even need to ask that?"

My insides squirm in embarrassment, because I wish I didn't. I wish I was as confident as I pretend to be. I wish all of the tattoos and piercings and asshole behavior that I use to push people away were actually enough to stop the constant craving for validation. I wish that my insecurity didn't gnaw at me as cruelly as it does. But I am still in awe that someone as interesting and bright as Blake even looked my way, let alone introduced me to their parents, so I answer, "Yes."

Blake takes a deep breath, before they answer in a gentle voice, "You tell me."

I groan out a laugh. "You're so annoying!"

"You did it to me first, Bud." Blake kisses my temple. "Go on, what impression do you think you made?"

I hold Blake tighter, as if I might merge into them, because everything always makes so much more sense when we're like this. Blake shines a light onto all the lies in my head, that are telling me that Michael ignored me because he doesn't think I'm worth talking to. That Linda kept asking so many questions because I was giving the wrong answers. That Matt and Allie kept jumping in because they saw I was floundering.

But knowing Blake, everything we've talked about the past month—since we basically switched from reluctant acquaintances to committed partners over the course of a weekend—everything they've shared about their family... The Ryans must have liked me enough to show me their real selves. Michael trusted Blake to know he could plug his ears and do his crossword puzzle, confident I wouldn't judge him or take it personally, with no need for him to make sure I was good enough for Blake. Linda asked questions because she was genuinely interested in what I had to say. Matt and Allie are just weak ass pushovers who are allergic to conflict, and I can tell that Linda and I will have many a debate in our future, if Blake still wants me around.

"It was fine, I guess," I eventually answer, overcome with appreciation that Blake lets me spiral for as long as I need to make my way back to center.

"More than fine," Blake wiggles down the couch a bit underneath me, so they can kiss my cheek instead of the top of my head. "They adored you, just like me."

"Hopefully not just like you," I tease, kissing their jaw. "Might make the next family gathering awkward if your parents are hitting on me."

Blake scoffs. "Fuck off, you know what I mean. They adored you, as much as, but not in the same manner as I do."

"You're so pedantic."

"Technically, *you* were pedantic that time."

"So your lease is up in September?" I ask, unsure if I want to start this conversation. Blake's new job is in Evanston. Right now, they're just a short train ride from me. But what if they move closer to work, and we don't see each other as often, or grow apart? What if this summer

is all we have? I could push this conversation off for later.
I could already be going down on Blake, giving them the
orgasms they've earned. But I can't help myself. "Do you
know what your plan is yet?"

Blake groans. "Yeah, end of September, but I don't
know what I'm gonna do. I spent three months apartment
hunting when I first moved here, and all I found in my
budget was that shitty studio."

"You're not going to renew?" I turn us on our sides,
so we're nose to nose in the quiet dark of my apartment.
My hand presses against Blake's back to keep them from
rolling off the couch.

Stretching out against me, Blake shakes their head.
"Every time I have to go back there, I dread it. It was fine
when I was in school, and I had class to go to and stuff, but
now? I shouldn't dread going home." They sigh, tracing
the scriptwork tattoo on my forearm. "But that reminds
me, I need to notify them I'm moving out. Even though I
don't know where I'll be living yet."

"You could stay here, if you want," I reply automatically.
My heart pounds as I realize what I've said, but I don't take
it back.

Blake's smile is distinctly smirk-like, but still so genuine—it takes everything not to taste it. "Bud, are you
asking me to move in with you? After a month together?"

Burning in embarrassment, I grumble under my breath,
"First of all, you brat, it'll be over three months by then.
And I'm not saying to move in permanently. Just, if you
need a place to stay in between leaving there and finding
a new place, this place is big enough for all of your books
and your mess." I clear my throat; the insecure part of me is
fighting what I'm about to say. "And...I would like to have

you here. Maybe after a while, if you can't find a place, and we both like how it's going, we can talk about that. But don't feel, like, pressured or whatever. I just want you to know, it's an option for you."

Blake's teasing smile stays put, even as their eyes soften—the big green eyes that went wide when we first met, then narrowed into a glare when I made some crass joke moments later. "You love me."

"What the fuck, Bambi," I groan, burying my face into the pillow. Of all the responses that could have come out of their mouth, that is just so Blake of them. We haven't... That word hasn't come up yet. Of course Blake would put it in my mouth, like stating a simple fact, as easy as anything.

Blake kisses my cheek, my neck, climbing onto my back to pepper me with kisses. "You *love* me," they singsong.

"Why are you like this?" I ask, wondering if my embarrassment will set the couch on fire.

"Because you like me like this," Blake murmurs, kissing my ear. "In fact, you *love* me like this. You have since the beginning. And I love you too, Eris."

I don't respond at first. I can't. My head is spinning at the direction this has taken. I need a moment to get my heart under control, before I say something rash or crude or mean that I'll regret. Ever since that second night in the hotel, since my meltdown in the bathroom at how overwhelmingly gone for Blake I was, I have been determined not to ruin this. Because I want this, want Blake, so much. The idea of losing them now? It hurts to think about.

But Blake is here, telling me they love me, giving me space to admit what we already know to be true.

Turning my head out of the blanket to face them, I look into Blake's eyes, still soft and warm and happy as they wait for me to stop freaking out. "Yeah. I do. I have, since the beginning."

Blake smiles, tracing my cheekbone with their finger before they kiss the tip of my nose. "Te amo, mi alma."

"Bambi," I murmur, melting into a giddy mess, even though their accent is trash. "Don't tell me you're learning Spanish."

Blake blushes at whatever they see in my expression. Considering I'm a flustered mess and already half-hard, they should be blushing. "Allie gave me some ideas for nicknames. Because Bambi can be so hot the way you say it, and Bud is incredibly unsexy, and I wanted a sexy nickname for you."

"You already have something hot to call me." My hand traces down their spine to the full ass I can never stop thinking about. I pull Blake's hips against me, so they can feel how much I'm enjoying this conversation. Blake's lips part in a gasp, and they curl around me. "Say 'Dámelo.'"

"Dámelo?" Blake wrinkles their nose. "I've never called you that."

I snort. "No, it's not a nickname. That's what you're going to say when you beg me to fuck you." I slide my hand down the front of their boxers, and as I expected, their hole is already soaking wet for me. "Poor Bambi, were you a needy mess all night?"

"You know I was, asshole." Blake rocks against my hand, trying to get me to touch their clit, but I sink my fingers into them instead. Eyes closing with a contented sigh, Blake goes limp in my arms. "You promised me orgasms, and we've been home forever, but I still haven't come once."

"I'll make up for it now, Bambi, I promise." I kiss them softly, but Blake's mouth is demanding, needy. As I flex my fingers deeper into them, they whimper around my tongue. "I owe you six, right? You'll get them all, you needy little slut, and more, as many as you can handle." I kiss them again as Blake shoves their joggers and boxers down their hips to give me more room. "What do you say when you want me to fuck you, Bambi?"

"Dámelo?" they reply, hesitantly.

"Dámelo who?" I prompt.

Blake frowns, pausing in their wiggling as they attempt to pull my dress over my hips. "Dámelo...Bud?"

There's no stopping the laugh that bursts out of me. Not even Blake's scoff of annoyance and push away from me that almost has them falling off the couch.

"Stop laughing at me!" Blake grumbles when I use the fingers inside them to roll them onto their stomach. Despite their annoyance, they shove a pillow under their hips and spread their thick thighs as far apart as they can with their joggers around their knees. I would sleep every night with my head cushioned on those pillows, if Blake let me. Soft and silky and plush, marred only by a few marks I've left over the past few days.

I press a kiss to one of those marks now, the perfect outline of my teeth on their ass cheek. "I'm not laughing at you, Blake, I promise I'm not. I'm laughing at how fucking sweet you are," I kiss the other cheek, "how unintentionally funny you are," another kiss to the small of their back, "what a fucking nerd you are."

With a smug smile, Blake looks back at me over their shoulder. "You're laughing at me because you *love* me?" They draw out the word, as if to tease me.

But I simply nod, kissing my way up their back. "Exactly. I'm laughing because I love you, so fucking much, Bambi." Blake practically preens under me as I hike up my dress, pulling my own drawers down. "Now try that again, but say my *name* this time, the way I like. Beg me to fuck you like the good little toy you are."

Blake wrinkles their nose, as if annoyed at themself for not realizing what I've been asking for the first time. "Dámelo, *Eris*."

I line myself up with their hole. "Say please."

"Dámelo, Eris," Blake smirks over their shoulder. "Por favor."

"Bueno, mi Bambi," I manage to say as I sink into them. Fucking Blake is the best high. Everything quiets between us, in my mind, in my heart. Anytime we're this close, everything feels easy. Blissful and relaxed under me, Blake gasps and moans and whimpers with each thrust. "Bueno, mi amor, mi vida, mi caracolito," I murmur as I fuck them, giving them as many nicknames as they might want, if they're so eager to try more out. So long as I'm their Eris and they're my Bambi.

As always, I am astounded and honored when Blake comes with a muffled shout into the blanket we're laying on, simply from me fucking them slowly. A surge of wetness soaks my thighs, and Dream is *never* getting this dress back. I have to fight to keep from coming along with them as Blake clenches around me, their orgasm making them shudder and moan underneath me. What the fuck did I do to deserve this? Like everything between us, this seems too easy to be real, but I appreciate each moment with Blake. How we're perfectly aligned, even with all our rough edges.

"What does that last one mean?" Blake asks when they can breathe again. I pull out, to give them a chance to come down before their next orgasm. "Cara, something? I recognized the rest, just not that one."

"Caracolito?" I snort, pushing their tee up to pat the photorealistic tattoo on their lower back. So fucking weird, but utterly magnificent. Just like my Bambi. "Little snail."

"Oh my god! Really? Snailito?" Blake wiggles away from me to roll onto their back. Perfect. I can kiss them when they're coming this time. That goofy crooked grin lights up their face as they look up at me. "I hate you."

"No, you don't." I finish tugging their joggers off their legs. Strange how after dinner, hours being anxious as fuck that I was going to ruin this, how easy this confidence comes to me. This is when all of this is simplest, just Blake and I alone together. When everything makes so much sense that it's laughable I would ever have doubts that we are perfect for each other. Hopefully, with enough time, patience, persistence...one day I might feel this way all the time. Crawling over them, I press a lingering kiss to Blake's lips. "You love me."

Familiar Faces

**A bridesmate who never remembers a face.
A groomsthem who is unfortunately forgettable.
A wedding night they'll cherish forever.**

ANANAS JACKSON HAS BEEN dreading xir sister's wedding from the moment Martina met her wonderful, charming fiancé, Mel. Martina deserves the utmost happiness, but this wedding means yet another major life change that Ananas isn't ready for. The only thing keeping xir from drowning is xir sister's support, the uptight mail carrier, and daily body-doubling livestreams; this wedding threatens any stability Ananas has. To make matters worse, xe's paired to walk down the aisle with Mel's college roommate—some stick-in-the-mud jerk xe's never met before, who won't look xir in the eye.

However, Kai insists they have met before. Many times, actually. While Kai is likely correct, Ananas doesn't exactly disclose xir prosopagnosia diagnosis to strangers, especially not pedantic nerds xe's forced to sit next to at the reception. Maybe if Kai was more interesting, Ananas would remember meeting them.

Little does Ananas know, Kai is as persistent as they are persnickety, and they accept Ananas's challenge. The night is young, neither of them brought a plus-one, and romance is in the air. Maybe this time, Kai will leave a lasting impression.

Book Two in the *Summer Weddings in Solberg* Series Coming May 2026!

Acknowledgements

This story was originally written for a Bi+ anthology: *Bi The Way, I Love You*, and I don't know if I would have written it at all if it weren't for the anthology. So huge thank you to Francis M. Thompson for organizing all of us into producing such a lovely anthology, and to my fellow contributors: Frances M Thompson, Amelia Lascaux, Julie Brydon, Rochelle Wolf, Madison Diaz, CJ Lucci, SC Muir, and MK Owens.

Thank you to my editor, Mikko Lahna at Quick Fox Editors, for your support with this project, your love of Eris and zis genderfuckery, and for laughing at my complete inability to flirt without accidentally hurting someone's feelings, just like Blake.

My deepest appreciation for Otte, my cover artist, who took my weird brief of "Can you draw a bouquet from this specific list of Minnesota wildflowers and cannabis, but leave the roots on and add snails and bugs?" and ran with it. Such a fabulous cover design, and one that really fits Blake so so so well.

To my many beta and sensitivity readers for this project: Thank you for loving my nasty freaks at all stages of their evolution.

To my friends from all stages of life, I am so grateful for those of you who have inspired some part of this story, from the random tattoos to finding your happily ever afters with fake wedding dates.

The *Bi The Way, I Love You* anthology was created as a fundraiser for Bi Pride UK and Rainbow Railroad. In that spirit of giving, the community aid beneficiary for the *Summer Weddings in Solberg* series will be Trans Lifeline, a community organization helping trans people survive and thrive. Find out more or make your own donation at https://translifeline.org/.

Also by Cozy

If you enjoyed this book (or if you didn't!), please kindly show your support by leaving a review and telling your friends about it. Honest reviews and word-of-mouth recommendations make it possible for indie authors to keep writing. Thank you!

Want to read more by Cozy? Check out their books at cozydubois.com

***Confession* Series**
Book 1: *Loving Lee*
Book 2: *Love on the Sunny Side*
Book 3: *Tempting Tara*
Book 4: *Carte Blanche*
Epilogue: *Finally Phineas* coming 2026!

Summer Weddings in Solberg
Petty Roots
Familiar Faces

Long Nights and Bright Futures
Glimmer in the Dark

Sleighbell Springs
For Luck's Sake

Short Stories
"Dad, Are You..." — part of *Bi All Accounts: Volume 1.*

About the Author

Cozy DuBois (they/them) thought writing fiction was a long-lost hobby. A longtime lover of romance novels, Cozy has renewed their love for writing by telling stories for and about LGBTQ+ people. They hope to bring more books into the world that represent the complex and entangled relationships between friends, lovers, and chosen family found in the queer community they love.

Based in Minneapolis, they enjoy life with their partner, two hound dogs, a regal queen of a cat, dozens of houseplants, and a garden that has seen better days. Find them with a beverage in hand on a patio anytime the temp is above freezing or planning their next vacation when it's not.

Connect with Cozy on social media or via email updates at cozydubois.com for announcements about upcoming releases.